D0033357

Colorado Cowboy
C.C. COBURN

HARLEQUIN®

TORONTO • NEW YORK • LONDON
AMSTERDAM • PARIS • SYDNEY • HAMBURG
STOCKHOLM • ATHENS • TOKYO • MILAN • MADRID
PRAGUE • WARSAW • BUDAPEST • AUCKLAND

Recycling programs
for this product may
not exist in your area.

ISBN-13: 978-0-373-75341-3

COLORADO COWBOY

Copyright © 2011 by Catherine Cockburn

This edition published by arrangement with Harlequin Books S.A.

For questions and comments about the quality of this book please contact us at Customer_eCare@Harlequin.ca

www.eHarlequin.com

Printed in U.S.A.

Cody sauntered back into the room

He returned after a good two minutes of making them all sit and wait on the edges of their seats. This kid really needed straightening out, Luke thought. He only hoped he was as up to the challenge as he claimed to be.

When Judge Benson explained to Cody what the adults had decided, he leaped to his feet and let loose with a string of colorful adjectives that had Megan blushing and begging him to stop. The judge sat there sagely, waiting for the tirade to end.

It eventually did and Cody threw himself into his chair. The room fell silent. "I'm not goin' anywhere," he snarled.

The judge sighed. "Then I'm afraid you give me no other choice, Cody." She picked up her phone and said, "I'll have to send you to juve—"

"I'll do it on one condition," he interrupted. Obviously there was room for negotiation where juvenile detention was concerned.

"And what might that be?"

"That he—" he pointed at Luke "—marries my mom."

It was hard to tell who gasped more loudly, Megan or Luke.

Dear Reader,

It is my pleasure to bring you the third installment of The O'Malley Men series.

You've met the oldest brother, Luke, in *Colorado Christmas* and *The Sheriff and the Baby* and I'm sure you've wondered just why Luke is so ornery. You'll find out in *Colorado Cowboy*.

Luke's world is turned upside down when he's summoned to New York to meet the teenage son he didn't know he had. A son in trouble with the law. Already the father of three adorable daughters, Luke can't get his son away from the mean streets of the big city and back to Colorado fast enough. There's just one little problem: Cody refuses to budge until Luke marries his mom!

I loved throwing challenges at Luke. The guy's virutally indestructible. He's the rock of his family and has suffered along the way, but will this final challenge break him?

I hope you enjoy reading Luke's story of how he adapts to life with yet another child, and how he and Megan fall in love. It's a bit of a back-to-front story in that Luke and Megan have a baby, get married and then fall in love.

I love hearing from readers. You can email me at cc@cccoburn.com. On my website, www.cccoburn.com, you'll also find photos of the Santa Maria ranch that helped inspire this story.

And please watch for firefighting brother Adam's story, coming soon.

Happy reading and healthy lives!

C.C. Coburn

ABOUT THE AUTHOR

C.C. Coburn married the first man who asked her and hasn't regretted a day since—well, not many of them. She grew up in Australia's Outback, moved to its sun-drenched Pacific coast, then traveled the world. A keen skier, she discovered Colorado's majestic Rocky Mountains and now divides her time between Australia and Colorado. Home will always be Australia, where she lives with her husband and two of her three grown children (the third having recently moved to England), as well as a Labrador retriever and three cats. But her heart and soul are firmly planted in Colorado, too. Her first book, *Colorado Christmas*, received glowing reviews and a number of awards. She loves hearing from readers; you can visit her at www.cccoburn.com.

Books by C.C. Coburn

HARLEQUIN AMERICAN ROMANCE

1283—COLORADO CHRISTMAS
1309—THE SHERIFF AND THE BABY

Acknowledgments

Many thanks to:

My fellow Harlequin American Romance author Cathy McDavid for her invaluable assistance in all matters to do with accounting.

Authors Karen Templeton and Katharine Swartz for their help with New York City.

Rancher Phil Craven of Texas. And George Meyers of the spectacular Santa Maria Ranch in Colorado—a true romantic, working hard to preserve the traditions of the West. Theoretical mathematician and sometime ranch hand and burro racer Daniel McCarl, for introducing me to George and showing me around the Santa Maria.

Sergeant Cale Osborn of Summit County Search and Rescue for his help with mountain rescue procedures.

And my dear friends equine veterinarian Dr. Holly Wendell and horse rescuer Helen Lacey for patiently educating me about horses.

Any errors or discrepancies in this story are the fault of the author and in no way reflect the expertise of the aforementioned.

Chapter One

Luke O'Malley didn't like the look of New York City one little bit. And he didn't like the look of his son any better.

The young street tough lounged in the judge's chambers, chewing gum and wearing an insolent expression. His contempt for everyone in the room extended to his unlaced sneakers braced against the judge's desk as he leaned back on the legs of his chair.

Last night, after receiving the call from the judge summoning him to New York to meet the son he'd fathered by Megan Montgomery, Luke couldn't help wondering: *Is this some sort of scam?*

Now a successful rancher, Luke employed innovative techniques at Two Elk, his ranch in the Colorado Rockies, which had ensured that his herds were among the best in the state, if not the West. And the horses he bred were of superior quality and in demand by ranchers and riders alike.

Had Megan seen the article about him in *Cowboys and Indians* a couple of months ago? He'd been swamped with letters from women looking for a rich husband, and he'd tossed them all in the trash. He wasn't interested in marrying a gold digger. He'd already been there, done that. Had no desire to repeat the experience.

For fifteen years, Luke had wondered about Megan, where she was, who she was with. Was she married? When he'd gotten the call from Judge Benson summoning him to New York, he'd gone. Even if the kid proved not to be his, he'd wanted to see Megan again with a need he couldn't explain. Ask her why she'd left so suddenly. Why she'd never answered the letter he'd sent to Wellesley.

Now she was back, and he wanted to touch her, kiss her, hold her. Make up for fifteen years without her. Fifteen years of trying not to long for her.

If there was any doubt in Luke's mind as to whether he had a son *before* he and his brother Matt walked into the judge's chambers this morning, they'd been dispelled the moment he laid eyes on Cody Montgomery. The kid was the spitting image of him and his brothers at the same age. Only the O'Malley boys hadn't dared wear their hair so long on one side that it covered their eyes. And on the other side…what the heck was with that buzz cut and the lightning strike shaved into it?

The O'Malley boys sure wouldn't have sported a thing like that miniature dumbbell stuck through their lip, chewed gum or peppered their conversation liberally with four-letter words, either. Their pop, Mac, had seen to that.

Nope. He didn't much like the look of Cody Montgomery, fourteen-year-old runaway and criminal-in-the-making. How had Megan let it come to this?

This is my so-called father? Cody thought. The guy acted like he had a pole stuck up his butt and Cody resented like the way he stared at him...especially his hair. And his lip piercing. Like he was some sort of freak. Okay, Cody wasn't so crazy about the lip piercing, either, but you needed it to look tough. To be part of the gang. Well, they weren't technically a gang—not yet, anyway. But the guys were checking around for one to join.

He hated the way the guy was looking at his mom, too. Like he didn't believe her. Like he didn't believe he was his son.

That just irritated Cody even more. How could *he* know who his father was? Whenever he'd tried to talk about it with his mom, she'd clammed up. Once, she'd said, "It was a mistake," but that only made it sound like she thought Cody was a mistake. *Worthless. Like trash.*

What else could he think? For all he knew, his real dad could be doing time. Or maybe what he'd done was even worse, though he couldn't think of anything much worse than having a criminal for a dad.

All the guys had fathers who were doing time, so Cody had pretended his was, too. He'd muttered something about armed robbery at a gas station when they asked about it.

Secretly, he hoped that if his father *was* doing time, it'd be for some minor crime, maybe some white-collar offense. That didn't hurt anyone—not physically, anyway. He wondered how many years you got for a white-collar crime. Probably less than fourteen...

He supposed it was okay if his father turned out to be some rancher from Colorado, like this guy claimed to be—as long as the guys didn't find out.

Cody had always liked the idea of Colorado. He

wondered if the guy lived anywhere near the Rockies.
He'd enjoyed reading *National Geographic* magazines
in the school library—when he was a kid. The pictures
of the Rocky Mountains were spectacular and somewhere he'd always wanted to go. Not that he'd ever admit
it. Now he didn't have time for that. Now he hung out
with the guys….

And now the judge was talkin' again! Sheesh!
Couldn't she just mind her own business for a change?
He was doing fine. He was surviving.

"…I therefore believe, Mr. O'Malley," she said, "that it
would be in Cody's best interests if he could be removed
from the environment he's living in at present—"

THE FRONT LEGS of Cody's chair hit the floor with a
thud as his feet came off the desk, and he spewed forth
a stream of invective that turned the air blue and had
Megan cringing in her seat. What must Luke think of
his son? What must he think of *her* for letting things
get this bad?

Judge Gloria Benson, as usual, was unperturbed.
She'd assured Megan at an earlier meeting that she'd
dealt with her share of juvenile offenders, plenty of them
a lot more hardened than Cody. A bit of bad language
didn't faze her. She'd told Megan that most of those
children—due to having families who didn't give a
damn—were beyond rescue, but she felt Cody had the
option of leading a better life.

The judge believed that with his father's interven-
tion, Cody had a good chance of making it to his next
birthday—unlike so many kids who came through her
court and didn't live past their teens.

That bald admission had been sobering for Megan.

The thought that her precious son might die before he reached adulthood… She'd wanted to pack them both up and catch a train or bus to anywhere that wasn't the Bronx or even New York City. Judge Benson had said, "I hope Mr. O'Malley has the courage to accept the challenge and follow through. Because right now, Cody's future is very precarious."

Considering the expression on Luke's face, he'd rather be anywhere than here with his son.

"Your honor," Megan said. "If you'd just give me another chance, I know I can put his life together and get him back into school."

"Ms. Montgomery…Megan…" Gloria sighed. Then she seemed to gather herself and said, "I can't tell you how many mothers have begged me for just one more chance before I send their child to juvenile detention. How many I've yielded to, and then weeks later heard their child had died in a gang fight, or from an over-dose of whatever drug was on the streets that day. I'm determined that's not going to happen to Cody. You're a good mom and I know you love your son. But unless you can afford to move out of your neighborhood to a better part of town, where Cody stands a chance of living a healthier—and longer—life, or we can find a solution here today, then I have no alternative but to send him to juvenile detention."

She turned her attention to Luke. "Cody's been in my court three times in as many weeks. His behavior is worsening. He's no longer attending school regularly. He's run away from home more than once, been caught joyriding in a stolen vehicle and I'm concerned he's on the brink of becoming part of the street gang culture of this city. Once that happens, he'll be lost to us."

Megan felt she had to explain, so Luke wouldn't see her as a complete deadbeat. "I'm working two jobs and in my final year of studying to be an accountant. I can't be there to watch him all the time," she said. But even as the words left Megan's mouth, she guessed the judge had heard that excuse far too often. In Megan's case, it was true.

"I understand all of that and your intentions are honorable," Judge Benson said. "But I'm afraid continuing the way things are will result in losing your son to crime and I know you don't want that."

Megan's tiny shake of her head was her only concession to her bald statement. She fought the tears that threatened and then lost the battle as they spilled down her cheeks and dropped onto her blouse.

The judge was right; she needed help with Cody, needed someone to take part in his care and discipline. "That's the reason I wanted to meet Cody's father and see if we could find a solution," Gloria explained. Obviously noticing Megan's distress, she opened a drawer, removed a box of tissues and offered them to Megan.

Megan's hands shook as she pulled several tissues from the box. Feeling thoroughly humiliated in front of Luke and his brother, she blew her nose and wiped her eyes and cheeks.

She wanted to turn her back on everyone. Protect herself from all the bad things in her life. Megan had never stopped loving Luke, in spite of his betrayal. She'd spent too many nights dreaming of seeing him again, being held, being kissed by him. Hearing him declare his love. Never once in those dreams had she imagined they'd meet under such humiliating circumstances.

Megan bit her lip, unable to meet the eyes of the rest

of the room's occupants, knowing everyone was staring at her. This would have to be about the lowest point in her life.

And then a warm hand covered hers.

How Megan had changed in fifteen years! Luke thought as he covered her hand, needing to reassure her she wasn't alone anymore.

He'd been a twenty-four-year-old ski-instructor attracted to the college junior with the twinkling blue eyes. She was on spring break in his hometown of Spruce Lake and, within days, they were dating. And then they'd made love. Several times. He'd guessed she was a virgin, but she'd been every bit as enthusiastic as he was. He'd fallen for Megan from the moment they met. It was only later that he wondered if she'd done it as a dare. A city-girl college bet—losing her virginity to the first cowpoke who came along.

She'd left Spruce Lake abruptly without even saying goodbye. He'd tried to contact her, but failed. Back then, cell phones weren't that common, not for college students, anyway.

Weeks later, he'd married his ex-girlfriend, Tory, because she'd claimed to be pregnant by him. He'd tried not to think about Megan for the past fifteen years.

Yesterday, when he'd received a phone call from the New York City judge informing him he had a son, he'd been shocked—disbelieving. To learn not only that he'd fathered Megan's child, but that his son was in trouble with the law, had left him numb and confused. Judge Benson had requested a meeting in her office. Her tone had brooked no argument.

He'd assured the judge that if the child was his, he'd

take responsibility and agreed to a meeting at noon the following day, anxious to resolve the matter, anxious to meet his son—if indeed this was his child. Anxious to see Megan again.

Paralyzed with shock, he'd turned to his brother, Matt, sheriff of Peaks County, for support. Matt had immediately agreed when Luke asked him to come to New York. They'd spent a sleepless night on the plane, discussing why Megan had never told him about the kid. How ironic that Tory had claimed to be pregnant with his child but wasn't, while Megan apparently *was*. How deeply he regretted allowing himself to be tricked by Tory, but at the time what was he to believe? They'd split up a few weeks before he'd met Megan. He had no reason not to believe her. If only he'd had the sense to demand a pregnancy test. But Tory had seemed so fragile, so lost…. She'd taken their breakup so badly he hadn't wanted to upset her any further.

He half wished Matt had worn his sheriff's uniform; maybe the kid would watch his language in the presence of an officer of the law.

And in spite of Matt's even-tempered counseling, Luke was still pretty steamed up by the time he'd arrived in the judge's chambers today. He wanted to know why Megan had kept something so important a secret. And how had things gotten to the point that his son was such a delinquent he was on a one-way trip to juvenile detention?

Most young women wouldn't hesitate to contact the father of their child, either to get money out of him—or pressure him to marry them—just as Tory had done. Yet Megan hadn't said a word.

He'd fallen so hard and so fast that, within a week

of meeting Megan, he'd wanted to make her his wife. She'd left him waiting at a restaurant with a diamond ring burning a hole in his pocket, feeling like every kind of fool when she hadn't shown up for their date that evening. Instead, Tory had. The woman was obsessed with him. Could find him anywhere in their small town. At first Luke was flattered, but he'd soon found it suffocating. That was why he'd broken up with Tory. However, the news she'd delivered that night guaranteed he'd be tied to her for a very long time. Bile rose in his throat at the memory and he made an effort to push all thought of his ex-wife firmly aside.

Megan had kept his son's existence a secret for more than fourteen years. Why? Luke had so many questions he needed answers to. He studied Megan, trying to gauge how she felt about being here. It was hard to tell, since she wouldn't meet his eyes. She sure seemed worn down by life. Her light brown hair had lost its shine and there were dark smudges beneath her once-vibrant blue eyes. She'd lost a lot of weight, too; her clothes almost hung off her thin frame.

"Luke?" Matt nudged him. "Judge Benson was speaking to you."

Luke turned back to the judge. "I'm sorry, Your Honor. I have to confess, this situation… Well, it's taking me a while to come to grips with it."

"Redneck!" Cody sneered.

"Cody, please?" his mother pleaded. "Don't speak to your fa—*Mr. O'Malley* like that."

That about sums it up, Luke thought. She's scared of the kid. Begging with him, for Pete's sake. So the kid figured his father was a bumpkin because he lived on a ranch, did he?

"I was saying, Mr. O'Malley, that it's taken a great deal of courage on Ms. Montgomery's part to reveal the name of Cody's father and allow me to get in touch with you.

"When I saw Cody here in court again the other day on yet another misdemeanor, I was deeply saddened. His mom is doing the best she can, but raising a child in a city like New York can be hard enough with two parents in the home. It's often almost impossible with one. And when that parent is finding it difficult to make ends meet, their children sometimes shoplift to get the things their parent can't afford to buy them. They're also easy prey for the street gangs. That will be Cody's future if I don't act now. My only alternative is to put him into juvenile detention—"

Cody swore, leaping to his feet, his chair clattering backward onto the floor.

"Cody! Don't use that sort of language. Apologize to the judge."

"No way!" he mumbled, picked up his chair and sat back down with a thud.

Luke was transfixed by the exchange. This kid didn't give a damn who he offended—or hurt—especially his mom. No wonder the kid assumed he could do what he wanted. She was incapable of disciplining him.

Cody leaned back in his chair, and Luke had a clear view of Megan. Tears were welling in her eyes as she looked at him, then glanced away.

She needed him. Needed someone to take charge—if only for a while.

Suspecting most of Cody's behavior was bravado—showing his father and uncle how tough he was—Luke knew one thing for sure: it was long past time to put a stop to it by starting to act like the kid's father.

He leaned toward Cody and said in a low growl, "A word. Outside." He stood and walked toward the door. The kid didn't move. *"Now!"* he said more harshly.

After several long beats, the kid got up and sauntered over to the door. He pushed past Luke and walked out into the foyer.

Thankful the area was deserted, Luke watched as Cody slumped against a column, crossed his arms and fixed a smirk on his face.

It took all of Luke's willpower not to grab his son by the shoulders and shake him. Instead, he took a deep breath and said, "I understand how angry you might be about the situation, but you won't speak to women in that way—*especially* your mother. Treat me how you want, but I will not allow you to *ever* treat your mother like that again."

"Yeah? How're gonna stop me?"

Apparently, the kid was expecting a physical threat, but that had never been Luke's way of disciplining his children. "Because I'm going to be your father from now on. You have a problem, you take it out on me, not your mom. Understand?"

He caught the flare of surprise in Cody's expression, then it became guarded again as he shrugged and said, "Whatever," and strode back into the judge's chambers.

He stood in front of the desk, arms still folded. "Can we go now?" he asked his mother.

"No, Cody, we're not leaving here until we've come to an agreement about your future."

Luke wanted to cheer. At last Megan had said *no.* Up

until now, all she'd done was try to placate her—*their*, he corrected himself—son.

"I think we're all agreed we don't want you in juvenile detention," the judge continued. "So now we need to decide on a solution. Sit down, Cody," she said firmly.

Cody hesitated for a moment and then complied, throwing himself into the chair and slouching in it, a sour look on his face.

Luke wasn't so sure juvenile detention *wasn't* the place for Cody. At juvie, they'd soon sort him out. His mom wouldn't have to constantly worry about where he was. Or maybe Luke could provide them with financial support. Then Megan wouldn't have to work; she could go to school full-time if she wanted. And he'd buy her a place in a better neighborhood.

"...my suggestion, therefore," the judge was saying.

Luke gave himself a mental shake.

"...is that for Cody's sake, he go and live with you on your ranch in Colorado—"

"*No!*" Megan cried.

Cody's predictable response was another four-letter word.

"You've got to be joking!" Luke exploded, incredulous the judge could suggest this young tough belonged on the ranch with his three innocent daughters.

She calmly folded her hands on her desk. "No, Mr. O'Malley, I'm deadly serious."

Luke shifted forward to emphasize his point. "I can support Cody *and* his mother. I'm more than willing to compensate her for the child support I should've contributed over the past fourteen years. Money isn't a problem."

"Oh, yeah! How much you gonna give me, *Dad?*"
The last word was loaded with derision.

"Cody!" Megan made eye contact with Luke for only
the second time since meeting again after so many years.
"I don't want your money," she snapped. "I can manage."
She turned desperate eyes to the judge and asked, her
voice trembling, "Are you saying you're giving Luke
custody of my son?"

The judge held up her hands and smiled compas-
sionately at Megan. "No, I'm not giving custody to Mr.
O'Malley."

Megan released a sigh of relief.

"I'm awarding you both custody. Joint custody."

There was another outburst from his son.

"Cody!"

Unflappable, the judge said, "Cody, if nothing else,
moving you to another environment might broaden your
vocabulary." She nodded at Luke. "Is this solution acceptable to you, Mr. O'Malley?"

Luke was horrified. It certainly was not. "Judge, I've
got three little girls. I don't want them exposed to this
sort of behavior—"

"Luke!" Matt muttered beside him.

His brother's caution made Luke realize how selfish
he was sounding. "I can pay to send him to boarding
school—get him out of this environment. That's what
you really want, isn't it? To get him away from the street
gangs? There are good boarding schools in Connecticut.
His mom could visit him on the weekends." He looked
at Megan, pleading for her agreement.

MEGAN WAS APPALLED by Luke's suggestion that they
send her son away to boarding school. But then she'd

relaxed when he mentioned she'd be close enough to visit Cody every weekend. Certainly a lot closer than Colorado. Maybe when Cody had settled down he could visit with Luke in Colorado. Get to know his father. It would tear her apart not seeing Cody every day, but this might be the only thing that would save him.

"I don't have any objection to an arrangement like that," she said, and glanced at Luke, then wished she hadn't. Feeling the familiar tug of attraction—but stronger now—she silently cursed her desire for this man. Fifteen years had only added to his dark good looks, but it was his willingness to bear some of the burden of raising Cody that had her reacting to him on such an elemental level.

She'd fallen for Luke within days of meeting him. She was so captivated by him, she'd gladly given up her virginity. He'd been charming and funny, with old-fashioned manners and beguiling brown eyes that made her heart melt and her common sense fly out the window. And what had her lapse in rationality gotten her in return?

The conversation she'd overheard at the recreation center the evening she was to meet Luke at the Victorian Inn for dinner had proven what a fool she'd been. He'd toyed with her emotions, stringing her along to believe they were in an exclusive relationship, when, in fact, the woman she'd overheard talking to a friend was pregnant with Luke's child.

She forced the anger—at herself and at Luke—aside and said, "I will agree to any solution that will get Cody away from the environment he's in at present. Somewhere safer, like a boarding school in Connecticut, would be acceptable to me—"

"I'm afraid that's not going to work," the judge cut in, then addressed Cody. "Would you excuse us for a moment, Cody? Your parents and I have things to discuss. You'll find refreshments and a television in the next room." She indicated a small door leading off her office.

Cody leaped to his feet. "Fine! Talk about me behind my back, why don't you? But I'm tellin' you now, I'm not goin' to any boarding school!" He stalked out, slamming the door behind him, causing Megan to jump with fright.

"I think as you can gather from that little tirade, Cody would only abscond from boarding school," the judge said. "And then we wouldn't know *where* he was."

Megan's earlier hope of getting Cody away from New York and the bad influences surrounding him plummeted. Judge Benson was right, of course. Short of enclosing him in ten-foot walls topped by razor wire, Cody would take off the second his supervisors' backs were turned.

CODY FOOLED AROUND, switching channels on the TV, his mind elsewhere, wondering what the adults in the next room were deciding about his life.

His *father* had other kids? Why hadn't his mom told him that? Maybe she didn't know until today, although by the look on her face, she wasn't that shocked. Maybe that was why his mom didn't want to talk about it whenever he'd asked. He was a married man and she'd had an affair with him. Yeah, that had to be it. His mom wouldn't do anything like that knowingly, so the guy must've lied.

He wondered what happened to his dad's wife, since

apparently she wasn't in the picture. Maybe he killed her and buried her on the ranch somewhere. He looked tough enough to kill someone. Judging by the death stare he kept giving him. *Yeah, you might think you're tough, old man, but you don't scare me!*

"CODY NEEDS A FATHER'S influence, and presence, badly," Judge Benson said. "Megan has spent fourteen years raising your son. It's now your turn to help with his upbringing. I appreciate your suggestion about the boarding school, but I think the best place for Cody right now is on your ranch in Colorado."

"No!" Megan cried. How could she even suggest such a thing? She'd never get to see Cody! It was as if her baby was being wrenched from her arms. Fighting tears, she appealed to the judge. "Cody is my life. My *only* family. You can't take him away from me, Judge Benson. Please don't do this to me."

"I'm not suggesting you stay here without Cody. I think it's best if you both move to Colorado."

The judge had to joking! "I can't do that. My life is here, in New York. I have job obligations and my study—"

Gloria Benson shook her head. "There's nothing to keep you here, Megan. No family, no worthwhile job. You can further your studies in Colorado. I'm suggesting that both of you try and make a go of being a family for Cody."

"But Luke has a wife. I'm sure she wouldn't want him spending his time between two families." She beseeched him with her eyes to tell the judge her plan wouldn't work. Why had the man been so silent throughout this discussion? Surely he was as upset as she was?

"I'm divorced," Luke said in a tone that had her staring at him in disbelief. Judge Benson hadn't said anything about that in the few minutes they'd had together before Luke arrived at the meeting. But she'd obviously been aware of it since she'd made such an outrageous suggestion. And then the impact of Luke's statement hit her. Luke was *divorced?* Somehow, that complicated things even more, but Megan couldn't put her finger on just why.

Matt cleared his throat and said, "I realize this is very difficult for you, Megan, but I'd like to say something on my family's behalf. We can all offer Cody a lot of support. We're a big, close-knit family with lots of positive male role models. I think Judge Benson's proposal is the ideal solution. There's plenty of room at the ranch for you and Cody, and you'd be most welcome there."

Luke rounded on him. "Hold it right there! I haven't agreed to anything. Can you honestly tell me that you want that…that—" he pointed toward the room Cody was in, glanced at Megan, then back at Matt, lowering his voice to a harsh whisper "—*juvenile delinquent* living under the same roof as your nieces?"

"He's not a *delinquent,*" Megan protested, her anger rising. How could Luke say that about his son? Be so callous about his own flesh and blood? If only he knew Cody better, he'd know he was a great kid. But since he didn't, she appealed to the judge. "Tell him Cody's a good kid. Please?"

"She's right, Luke. Cody *is* a good kid. He was getting excellent grades in school until a few months ago, but a bad element has moved into the area and it's negatively affecting some of the kids. That display he subjected you to is simply bravado. It's going to take some work to get him back again. Hard work." She played her trump card. "I was hoping you'd be up to it."

Megan felt her lip curl. Luke hadn't been man enough to acknowledge he had a son fourteen years ago when she'd sent him a letter just after Cody's birth, telling him she'd had his child. If he couldn't accept then that he had a baby, he certainly wouldn't be up to the challenge of raising a difficult teen now.

She blinked back tears as she remembered that sad time. The letter going unanswered. The phone call she'd made to the ranch a month later—just in case he hadn't gotten her letter. It had been answered by a woman. Megan had given her name and asked to speak to Luke, but the woman had said, "Luke's away at a convention. I'm his wife. Shall I tell him you called?"

Shocked to the point of gasping for air, Megan had hung up. *Luke was married.* So the conversation she'd overheard hadn't been a mistake or a figment of her imagination. Megan had never felt lonelier than at that moment. Nor had she ever felt more foolish. She wasn't contacting Luke to get money out of him, and she didn't expect him to play a part in their son's life—not if he didn't want to. She'd written the letter as a courtesy. Whether he'd received it or not, there was no point in leaving a message with Luke's wife.

"Megan, are you all right?"

Judge Benson's voice broke into her thoughts and Megan made an effort to control her emotions. She didn't want anyone in this room to know how vulnerable she felt, to know the truth of how stupid and gullible she'd been. Or how angry she was with Luke for denying their son back then.

LUKE TRIED TO CONVINCE himself it was worth risking the stable family life he'd worked so hard to restore since Tory deserted them, only to turn it upside down by letting Cody into it. He wished he'd known about his son all those years ago. Megan was seriously delusional if she thought Cody wasn't a delinquent. Otherwise, why were they all here?

"I know my brother is more than able to rise to the challenge, Judge." Matt's foot connected with Luke's ankle. "I think he's just a little stunned to find out he's a father again. Aren't you, Luke?"

Luke sent his interfering brother a glare. He was perfectly capable of making up his own mind; he didn't need Matt making it up for him. "I'm prepared to give it a try…if Megan is." He looked across at her, his eyes begging her to disagree. She lifted her head defiantly. If he wasn't mistaken, that was pure loathing in her eyes.

As if to thwart him, she gave an almost imperceptible nod.

"I don't want you going into this halfheartedly, Mr. O'Malley." The judge's voice held steel. "What we have here is a boy in desperate need of a father's influence and a strong family relationship—and a mother who's willing to agree to that."

Luke shot another glance at Megan. She didn't look too willing.

"What I need from you is a commitment to your son. A commitment that you will *not* fail him. He needs you, more than he's ever needed anything in his life. And believe me, we *are* talking about his life."

The judge's sobering words brought Luke up short. If Cody continued as he was, his life could be in danger.

Sending him away to boarding school wasn't the answer.

He squared his shoulders. "You have my promise, Judge. I'll do everything within my power to help Cody. I'm committed to being his father in every way possible."

The judge nodded and sat back, visibly more relaxed. "Good. So you'll move to Colorado, Megan?"

"If that's what you think is best," Megan said stiffly. Hands clasped, she avoided Luke's gaze.

"Yes," Judge Benson said. "But now we have to face the hard part." She picked up the phone and addressed her assistant. "Would you ask Cody to step back in, please?"

CODY SAUNTERED BACK into the room after a good two minutes of making them all sit and wait on the edges of their seats. It was this sort of insolence that Luke would never tolerate from his daughters. The kid really needed straightening out. Luke only hoped he was as ready for the challenge as Matt claimed he was. He had enough stress in his life, and adding a troubled child to the mix wasn't going to help.

When Judge Benson explained to Cody what the adults had decided, he scrambled to his feet and let loose with a string of colorful adjectives that had Megan blushing and begging him to stop, Luke ready to leap from his chair, drag him to the bathroom to wash out his mouth and both Matt and the judge sitting sagely, waiting for the tirade to end.

Eventually it did, and Cody threw himself back into his chair. The room fell silent. "I'm not goin' anywhere," he snarled.

The judge sighed. "Then I'm afraid you give me no other choice, Cody." She picked up her phone and said, "I'll have to send you to juve—"

"I'll do it on one condition," he interrupted. Obviously, there was room for negotiation where juvenile detention was concerned.

"And what might that be?"

"That he—" Cody pointed at Luke "—marries my mom."

It was harder to tell who gasped louder, Luke or Megan.

MEGAN FOUND HER VOICE first. "Cody! What are you saying?"

He glared at her, chilling Megan to the bone. What had become of her once sweet-natured son?

"If you want us to play 'happy families,' then he's going to have to marry you. And I mean *right now*." He gestured dismissively at Luke. "I want him to be committed to us. I don't want him hanging around and pretending to be my dad, like what happens to the other kids in the neighborhood, and then have him run off when somethin' better comes along."

"We'll be living in Luke's home, Cody," she reminded him. "He won't be going anywhere."

"You know what I mean!" he cried, jumping up and overturning his chair. "Everyone in our neighborhood's had dozens of 'dads' or 'uncles' living with them. None of 'em ever stay around for long 'cause they're not married to the kids' moms. They don't care. They're only there for the sex!"

"Cody!" Megan was horrified. Yes, it *was* like that in their neighborhood, but she'd never had another man stay the night, let alone *live* with them. She hadn't even dated. She glanced at Luke to guess what he must be thinking. Did he believe she'd had a succession of men through the door like some of the other single moms in their neighborhood? The men got all the fringe benefits but took none of the responsibility, and they left when things got hard. Or they went to prison.

Luke was watching her carefully, as though considering her reaction, but Megan couldn't think of a thing to say to dispel the notion that she was one of those unfortunate women.

LUKE SEARCHED CODY'S features. Was the kid trying to manipulate the adults in the room? Or did he genuinely feel that without a marriage certificate, their "family" wouldn't be a valid one?

"It's not going to be like that, Cody. I have a big house. Your mom and you can have your own space. What I'm offering is the security of a home and family who'll love you and care about you."

"How can I know you mean that if you don't care enough about me to marry my mom?"

Luke could see through the bravado to the pain in Cody's eyes. The kid had been through the wringer. Lord knows what kind of men must've been in his life for him to question Luke's commitment like this. Cody wasn't asking them to live as husband and wife and sleep in the same bedroom—and judging by the sparks of anger emanating from Megan, that wasn't even a remote possibility.

What his son was doing was asking Luke to prove he cared about *him,* to prove he'd stick around—by marrying his mom. It was a hell of a big demand, but his son's immediate future was more important than Luke's need for a wife he loved, a wife who'd warm his bed at night. And by marrying Megan, that was what he'd be doing— sentencing himself to a loveless, celibate marriage.

Cody was too young to understand how complex marriage was, how deep the commitment needed to be for both parties to make it work. He'd been twenty-four when he'd married Tory, and at that age he hadn't understood it himself.

"You can't make demands like that Cody," he said as gently as he could. "What you're asking isn't fair to either of us. Your mom has agreed to Judge Benson's suggestion that you both come and live on my ranch. Let's leave it at that."

Cody crossed his arms and nestled further into his chair. "If you won't marry her, I'd rather go to juvie than live on your hick ranch."

"No!" Megan cried, turning to him. "Don't joke about that."

"I'm not joking, Mom. I *mean* it. I need to know he cares enough about me to marry you. He should've done it fifteen years ago."

Luke winced at that. If he'd known about Cody, he would've married Megan. But she hadn't given him that chance and he'd been robbed of knowing his son, of guiding him toward becoming a man. He looked at Cody. The kid was truly hurting. Hurting inside and hurting his mom in the process.

Megan's eyes held terror as she appealed to him. "Please...*do something*," she begged. "He means what he says. He'll go to juvenile detention and I'll lose him forever!" Megan covered her face and turned away.

Luke watched Cody's reaction to his mom. Initially,

the kid seemed upset that his mother was in so much pain, and then he got a grip on himself and set his mouth in a firm line—a look Luke associated with his younger brothers at a similar age, when they'd decided they were going to do something and nothing and no one was going to stop them. Cody glared back at Luke as though it was all his fault Megan was crying. All Luke's fault that he hadn't given him his name and his birthright. The love of a father and a family.

Cody was fourteen now, far from being a man. Luke determined there and then that by the time Cody was eighteen, he'd have turned the boy's life turned around, instilled in him what it was to be a responsible member of the community. A man. By then Cody would be graduating from high school and heading off to college. So what was sacrificing four years of his life for the betterment of his son's? If he married Megan now, in four years, they could divorce, move on, find other partners. But in the meantime, Cody would have time and space to grow up and become a contributing member of society. If he went to juvenile detention, his son's life could be in more danger than Luke would allow himself to imagine.

Megan sat with her head down. She looked so vulnerable, so desperate to do the best for their son, but would she agree to such an outrageous proposal? Luke knew he was probably going to make the second biggest mistake of his life—but it might be the only decision that would save Cody.

Sick with fear for his son, Luke got up and went to stand in front of Megan. She refused to lift her gaze to his, so he crouched down.

"Megan," he murmured, waiting until her head came up and she'd focused her sad, defeated eyes on him. Then he asked, "Will you marry me?"

Chapter Two

Luke stared out the window of the airplane as it flew west, home to Colorado. He couldn't believe what he'd done. Within minutes of proposing to Megan, the judge had them standing before her, reciting their vows.

He'd taken along his birth certificate and ID to the meeting as requested. Apparently the judge had asked the same of Megan. Gloria Benson had issued a marriage license and then, using her judicial powers, had waived the normal thirty-day waiting period required in New York State.

Matt wore a grin from ear to ear throughout the short ceremony. Megan frowned at Luke and chewed her lip while Cody had looked totally bewildered that they'd gone along with his ultimatum. The fact that they'd managed to completely catch him off guard was the only high point of the ceremony. Megan had turned her cheek aside when the judge had pronounced them husband and wife and invited Luke to kiss his bride.

If Luke had thought his marriage to Tory was a living hell, he was having genuine misgivings about marrying a woman who loathed him so much. At least Tory had pretended to like him—for a while.

Four hours later, after arranging to have Megan's

and Cody's possessions packed by a moving company and sent to the ranch, they were on the flight to Denver. Cody had protested that he wanted to go home and get some things, but Luke had refused to let him anywhere near their old neighborhood and instead had taken him shopping for new clothes. That, if nothing else, had earned Cody's grudging agreement. Megan had purchased a few items to tide her over, too.

"Thank you," she'd said quietly as they waited at the curb outside the department store for the cab to take them to the airport. It was the first time she'd spoken to him since the ceremony.

Luke looked at her, puzzled.

"Thank you for giving my son a chance." For once she wasn't looking at him with barely disguised hatred in her eyes.

"He's *our* son," he'd said. "We *will* make this work— together." And then he'd spotted the jeweler's window, turned to Matt and said, "Can we meet you back here in fifteen minutes?" He took Megan's elbow and led her to the window. This might be a marriage of convenience and Megan might hate his guts—although Luke was at a loss to understand why—but a ring was symbolic and, right now, that was all this marriage had going for it.

"Choose a ring," he'd said.

"Luke, this isn't necessary. We've been through the motions. I think that's all Cody really wanted." She smiled tightly. "In fact, I think he's as shocked as we are."

Luke couldn't help grinning. "He is, isn't he? Maybe we should surprise him every so often by agreeing to some outrageous idea."

"Careful," she warned. "He's got an active imagination."

Luke hadn't let go of her elbow and he gave it a little squeeze, needing to impart a sense of mutual purpose. "I'm sure at heart he's a good kid, Megan. We can do this."

She nodded as though resigned to their situation. "I'm determined to."

Luke had followed her into the jewelry store. An assistant showed them the wedding rings, and Megan selected a plain gold band for Luke. "The girls will like this," he said. "Okay, let's get something special for you."

"I'd completely forgotten about your little girls. How are they going to feel about this? You coming home with a wife *and* a son. It's going to be an awful shock for them."

"They'll probably insist we get married all over again for their benefit."

Megan bit her lip. Luke didn't want to find it endearing, but it reminded him of her so long ago….

"Never fear, we have our very own judge in the family. Becky will rise to the occasion with a far more romantic event than our first wedding. If that's what you'd like."

Megan blushed and looked back at the rings, and Luke drew his cell phone out of his pocket. "You keep doing that. I'm just going to call my girls and let them know what's going on."

Luke had turned away from Megan to make his call in private. Fortunately, he got hold of Matt's wife, Beth, rather than one of his daughters. Matt had apparently called Beth already and explained the situation.

"Congratulations, Luke! I don't know anyone who's gained both a son and a wife in one day before."

"Very funny," he said. "Can you put one of the girls on, please? I feel I need to warn them."

"Lucky for you, Sash isn't home at the moment. But Daisy's here. I'll put her on."

Luke grimaced as he waited for Daisy. Beth was right, Sash probably wasn't going to be happy at the news of his marriage. She was full of teenage angst and hormones, and these days it was more likely she'd be in a bad mood than a good one.

"Hi, Daddy!"

"Hey, squirt," he greeted his middle daughter, Daisy.

"When are you comin' home?"

"Tonight, honey, but first I need to tell you something."

THE CALL COMPLETED, Luke had closed his phone and turned to Megan. He hoped he hadn't said anything on his end to give any indication that things mightn't be rosy back at the ranch at the news of their marriage.

"How about that one?" she asked.

He shook his head. "Too plain. Hey, that's nice." He pointed to a diamond-encrusted gold band.

"It looks like an engagement ring," Megan said.

"No, madam," the assistant remarked. "It's a special design that incorporates the engagement and wedding rings in one design."

"I like it," Luke said. "It suits us. We got engaged and married at the same time."

When Megan had looked up at him and blinked, Luke experienced a rush of protectiveness toward her. She seemed as full of wide-eyed innocence now as she had nearly fifteen years ago. If only he'd realized back then how much their actions would change their lives...

"I guess you're right. Okay," she said.

The assistant had removed the ring and passed it to Luke, who raised Megan's hand and placed it on her finger, holding his breath and hoping it fit. It really was a beautiful ring and symbolic of their hasty engagement and marriage. "Perfect," he said when it fit. He looked into her eyes, trying to see what was hidden there.

She'd blushed and pulled her hand away. "We'd better get back. They'll be wondering what's happened to us."

Luke nodded. There'd been something in her eyes, something strange and unreadable. He planned to get answers when they were alone at the ranch—starting with why she'd kept Cody's existence a secret.

He'd quickly paid for the rings and, as they didn't need wrapping, headed outside to find Matt and Cody still waiting, only now Cody was wearing headphones attached to a handheld gaming device he was absorbed in playing.

"Cody! Where did you get that?" Megan cried, as though fearing he'd stolen them.

"Relax." Matt placed a restraining hand on her arm before she pulled the headphones off and repeated her question. "Cody suggested we pop back into the store. Somehow I got talked into buying him that."

"I'm so sorry, Matt," Megan said. "I...I'll pay you back as soon as I can."

"Megan, he's my nephew and I owe him a bunch of birthday and Christmas presents. Besides, it's a long trip back to Denver and this is a small price to pay for some peace and quiet. He hasn't uttered a single curse since he put them on."

"Really?" Megan's frown turned into a smile, lighting up her face. Luke liked the effect.

Luke hailed a cab, which whisked them to the airport. Since it was a Friday, the flight was full, but fortunately there were seats available in first class. Luke purchased them without batting an eye.

Cody had seemed impressed and set about devouring every item of food offered to him. He'd then downed a couple of sodas and fallen asleep.

Luke glanced across the aisle at his sleeping son and felt a pull of recognition. He was an O'Malley all right. In spite of the hair and the piercing, he resembled the O'Malley males. He was already pushing six feet and would no doubt end up at least as tall as Matt, who at six-four was the tallest of the five brothers and two inches taller than Luke. Matt, too, was sleeping. How alike his son and his brother looked. Cody had the square, sometimes stubbornly set jaw and straight nose that characterized the O'Malleys.

It was so strange to discover he had another child. A son. He wondered how the girls were going to take it. Twelve-year-old Sasha would probably hate him on sight—and not hesitate to say so! She was at that difficult age—no longer a girl, not yet a woman—with a mass of confused hormonal behavior to back it up. Nine-year-old Daisy, in spite of her feminine name, would challenge him to an arm wrestling or calf-tying contest. She was a real tomboy and loved ranch life. Sweet four-year-old Celeste would have him wrapped around her little finger in minutes.

A pang of conscience gripped him. Was he taking a

huge risk by exposing his very innocent, country-raised daughters to his tough, streetwise son? He hoped not and then wondered what Cody would make of his half sisters.

He looked at Megan, dozing beside him, her seat reclined. With her face relaxed in sleep, he could see the beauty that had first attracted him fifteen years ago.

Whoa there, fella! Megan Montgomery might be his wife of a couple of hours, but he hadn't thought about her *that* way in a very long time. She'd been a holiday fling that had turned into something deeper—or so he'd believed until she'd run out on him. He'd had a lot of flings while working as a ski instructor. The job had provided an income over the winter months while his father tended the ranch. Luke was well aware when he started dating Tory that she'd had several lovers. But so had he. She was a willing bed-partner and he didn't think beyond that because he didn't intend to make their relationship permanent. When Luke married Tory a month after Megan left town, he'd hung up his instructor's jacket and given up the carefree bachelor life for good.

Megan stirred and shifted, moving her head closer to him. She breathed in deeply, then exhaled a tiny sigh and buried her head against his arm.

Luke sat stiffly, waiting for her to settle, fighting his reaction to the sound of that tiny, innocent sigh and the feel of her nose pressing against his arm.

This wasn't what he'd planned. He'd assumed he could remain cool and aloof, treat Megan with the respect due the mother of his child and not get involved.

He stood and made his way to the bathroom.

MEGAN FELT LUKE LEAVE his seat, felt the warmth leave her body where her face had nestled against him. She'd woken herself up with that sigh of contentment. Woken up after having a wonderful, slightly erotic dream that even *smelled* good. And then she'd opened her eyes and realized where she was—on an airplane with her face right up against Luke's arm. He was wearing a polo shirt so she'd been burrowed against his bare, muscled flesh. She hadn't dared move, in case he saw she was awake.

"Would you care for a drink?" the flight attendant asked.

Startled, she sat up. "What? Um, I guess so." Unaccustomed to the luxury of flying first class, Megan was a little intimidated by the attentive service. Once, a lifetime ago, such treatment was what she'd been raised to expect.

"We'll have a bottle of your best champagne," she heard Luke saying as he returned to his seat.

The flight attendant turned toward Luke and stepped a little too close for Megan's liking. "Celebrating something?"

"We just got married today."

"Oh, that's lovely," she said, although it sounded to Megan like she didn't really think that was lovely at all. "Congratulations." She encompassed Megan in her already faded smile. "I'll get a bottle and two flutes immediately, sir," she assured Luke.

Luke stretched and then sat down. "I hope you don't mind. It seemed appropriate. We haven't had a chance to toast each other and our future together."

Our future. She wondered how long that future could possibly last. Luke wouldn't be satisfied with hanging around home and hearth indefinitely. He'd soon be out seeking the company of other women. Willing women like the young flight attendant. Sadness engulfed her. Sadness and confusion. She could never hope to compete for Luke's affections with such a smorgasbord on offer. But was that what she actually wanted? Luke's affections? A real marriage—to him? Too much had happened in too short a time; her life had changed in a matter of hours and she hadn't caught up to it yet.

"Is everything okay?" Luke asked.

"What? Oh, yes. Fine. Why?"

"You look a little peaked. I hope you're not having regrets already."

Not yet, but I know I soon will, she thought.

"You're afraid of heights. Are you also afraid of flying?" he asked, reminding them of their first date.

Luke had packed a picnic and driven them to Inspiration Point, a local beauty spot above the town of Spruce Lake. The location would've been ideal—if it didn't plunge nearly a thousand feet to the valley floor. As soon as she'd stepped from his vehicle and noticed how high they were and just how close the cliff face was, she'd suffered an attack of vertigo and nearly passed out.

Interesting that he'd remembered that date…and how afraid of heights she was.

To purge the memory of Inspiration Point from her mind, she said, "Tell me about your daughters, Luke, and the rest of your family. I remember you're the oldest of five boys and that you were all raised on a ranch, but I guess in the few weeks we…knew each other, that's all I ever found out about you."

The champagne arrived, and Luke allowed the flight attendant to pour the sparkling liquid into two chilled flutes.

He turned toward Megan and touched his glass to hers. "To us."

She lifted the glass to her lips, took a sip, then crinkled her nose and sneezed. "Oh! The bubbles got to me," she said. "I'm sorry. I didn't mean to spoil your toast."

He touched his glass to hers a second time and said, "Let's try that again."

They did, and Megan managed to keep her ticklish nose under control.

She settled back against the seat and listened while Luke filled her in on his family, loving the sound of his voice, deep and sure. She'd done the right thing letting the judge get in contact with Luke. Who was she kidding? She hadn't had any choice. Judge Benson had practically blackmailed her into it! Either she gave her Luke's details, or Cody would be sent to juvenile detention that very night.

It'd been easy to get Luke's number. He'd been at the ranch his family had lived on for four generations. Megan had asked to leave before the judge spoke to him. She didn't want to be in the room and hear Judge Benson going through a long explanation of who Megan was and hearing him deny that he knew her, hearing him insist he couldn't possibly have fathered her child. The denial would've hurt too much.

When Judge Benson called Megan that night, she'd told her Luke was arriving the next day and they'd be meeting in her chambers. Stunned by the swiftness of his response, she'd asked, "Did he remember me?" and instantly cursed herself for sounding so desperate, so *adolescent*.

It gave her a tiny thrill when the judge said, "Of course he does, Megan. He seems like a very pleasant man, if a little dazed at the news that he has a son. He'll be in my chambers tomorrow at noon. Please be there with Cody."

"Of course I will. And, Judge Benson, thank you so much for taking the time to care about Cody."

"It's my pleasure, Megan," the judge had told her. "At this point, as I explained to you earlier, I think the best thing for him is to meet his father. I'll take it from there."

"H-how do you know that's the best thing. You haven't met Luke. He could be an ax murderer or… or—"

The judge had laughed heartily. "An ax murderer with a voice like that and a glowing character reference from both the local sheriff *and* a county judge? I don't think so. See you at noon tomorrow."

The judge had hung up before Megan got a chance to question her further. Megan hadn't slept a wink.

"…then there's Matt. He's married to Beth."

Megan was brought back to the present, wondering how much she'd missed of what Luke had said.

"Are you sure you're okay?" Luke asked. "You were looking at me, but I don't think you were taking much in."

"I…I guess I'm just tired." She shrugged. "Jet lag."

"It's only 6:00 p.m. New York time. You can't be *that* tired."

Luke held his hand to her forehead. She told herself not to think anything of it. His apparent concern probably meant as much now as it had back then. *Nothing.*

Luke took the champagne glass out of her hand and pressed the flight attendant call button. When the woman appeared, he handed her the glass and said,

"My wife isn't feeling well. Could you get her a cool compress."

My wife. The words had Megan's heart pounding. They sounded so good. So...*possessive.* Normally, she would've backed away from such a notion. But those words—coming from Luke—had sounded...like something she very much needed to hear.

"I'm fine," she assured him. "I'm just a little tired. I didn't sleep well last night." Megan wished she could take that statement back, not wanting Luke to know she'd been terrified about today's meeting.

But if she was honest with herself, she'd liked his take-charge attitude. She'd especially appreciated it when he'd dealt with her boss at the supermarket where she stocked shelves each evening. When Luke had asked for the phone numbers of her workplaces, she'd had to explain, embarrassed to the core, that she'd been fired from her job at a call center that morning. Her boss there had been unwilling to give her time off so she could attend the meeting at Judge Benson's chambers, claiming he'd cut her too much slack already over her son. Furthermore, her boss at the supermarket had told her that if she was late for work one more time, she'd be looking for another job.

This morning, she'd been frantic, worrying how she'd pay the rent if she lost not just one job, but two. She'd been mortified as she told Luke, watching his face crease—with disgust.

She'd thought the disgust was aimed at her until he'd pulled out his cell phone, dialed the number she gave him and told Jerry at the supermarket that his wife, Megan *O'Malley,* was moving to Colorado that day and therefore wouldn't be reporting for work that evening.

She could hear Jerry sputtering on the other end of the phone. Luke had cut him off with a sharp, "You threatened to fire Megan if she got to work late this evening. This is a courtesy call to let you know she won't be in tonight—or any night." Luke had then given him a post office box number to send her paycheck to and impressed on her ex-boss that he expected the check to arrive within the week; otherwise, he'd be taking action. After repeating virtually the same threat to Pat Reagan at the call center, Luke closed his phone and smiled at her. "I hope you don't mind, but I won't have you fired from two jobs in one day."

"Better for me to quit at least one of them?" she'd asked, still a little stunned by what Luke had done.

"Exactly. I have a feeling your self-esteem has taken quite a battering over the past months. I'm going to help change that."

At that promise, Megan started to fall a little in love with him all over again. Although she'd fought her own battles over the years, it was heaven to have someone in her corner for a change. And Luke was right about her self-esteem. It had never been particularly high, but having to work menial, minimum-wage jobs to make ends meet, while pursuing her studies, had caused her sense of worth to plummet. To further realize that all her sacrifices to provide a better life for her and her son were amounting to nothing made her feel as if she was on a nosedive to nowhere.

The flight attendant reappeared, handed the compress to Luke. He placed it on Megan's forehead. "This should help," he said. "Now, close your eyes and get some sleep."

She forced herself to breathe deeply and slowly,

allowing each part of her body to relax. She succumbed to sleep, her last conscious thought: *What happens tonight?*

LUKE WATCHED MEGAN SLEEP, feeling a protectiveness toward her he'd never felt for Tory.

Even when Tory had supposedly miscarried months after they married, he hadn't felt anything for her. He should have ended the marriage then, when she'd claimed to lose the baby, but Tory had threatened suicide, so he'd stayed, feeling responsible for her.

It wasn't until many years later that he discovered Tory hadn't been pregnant. He'd been such a fool, allowing Tory to dupe him into marrying her.

Luke turned his attention to Megan, determined to purge any thoughts or regrets about Tory from his mind.

She sure was different from the girl he'd known nearly fifteen years ago. Back then, if the bubbles had gotten up Megan's nose, she would've giggled and asked for more. She wouldn't have apologized for anything. What had made her change? She seemed so unsure of herself. She'd been an economics undergrad back then. He'd been under the impression that she came from a wealthy family, since she was attending Wellesley College, wore a Rolex and her ski suit, boots and skis were top-of-the-line. She and her friends were staying at Spruce Lake's most expensive hotel, where the rooms went for more than a thousand dollars a night.

Luke sighed with disgust at himself. He'd chosen the Victorian Inn for the dinner where he'd intended to propose, because it was the most expensive in the county. He'd expected her to be impressed. Never mind that the bill would cost him at least two weeks' pay. Megan was worth it.

So, what had happened to all the wealth? he wondered. Had her parents lost everything in a stock market or property crash? He wanted to ask, but it seemed too intrusive a question.

The only thing that really mattered was that she was back in his life. Sure, he was angry, wanted answers as to why she'd kept Cody a secret, but there was time enough to deal with that. Luke was confident that once she'd settled in at the ranch, he and Megan could take up where they left off. Become lovers again. But first, they had to become friends.

"WE'RE HERE." LUKE'S DEEP voice broke into Megan's dreams.

Megan opened her eyes to find Luke leaning over her and thought she wouldn't mind waking up like that every day for the rest of her life.

"We're coming into Denver. You'll have to put your seat upright," he said, pressing the button on her armrest. "You've had a long sleep."

Megan was having trouble separating fantasy from reality. She felt drugged and shook her head to clear it. It couldn't be the champagne; she'd only taken a few sips.

The plane touched down and the pilot made his announcement about local time. Megan turned her watched back two hours, to just after 6:30 p.m. Then she looked across to check on Cody. It was the first time he'd been on a plane, but he hadn't displayed a second's concern about it. In fact, he was talking animatedly to Matt and pointing out the window at the huge airport terminal they were taxiing toward. He'd even removed his ear-plugs from his ears. Usually Cody wouldn't give an adult the time of day and would've ignored all attempts to engage in conversation, but Matt seemed to have the magic touch.

She smiled and said, "I can see an improvement in Cody already."

"Matt's got a way with kids." His mouth turned down in a slight grimace. "I wish I had his easy way of dealing with them. Especially my son."

Megan couldn't begin to imagine the regrets Luke must be having. He'd not only taken on a wife and a recalcitrant son but also a stepmother to his daughters and a half brother to them, as well. She wondered how the little girls would react to the changed family structure. Would they accept it? Or would they rebel? Megan shuddered. She knew exactly what her son's reaction would be in those circumstances.

"Relax. Everything'll be fine," Luke said, correctly guessing her thoughts.

Megan bit her lip. "I wish I had your confidence."

When the plane stopped at its gate, Luke removed their carry-on luggage from the overhead bins. An overnight bag for him and a couple of department-store shopping bags for Megan. He stood back to let her exit the plane ahead of him.

Since Cody had several department-store bags stuffed full of clothes Luke had bought him, they'd purchased an overnight bag at the airport, to save any problems with security. He watched as Cody drew out his bag and stuffed in the toiletry wet packs, usually reserved for overseas segments, that he'd talked the flight attendant into giving him.

Luke ignored the transgression. He figured he'd paid enough for the four seats to warrant a few souvenirs. He smiled down at Megan, warning her with a shake of his head not to protest. "At least we won't be held up at the baggage carousel," he said. Their cabin luggage was all they had to take with them.

TWENTY MINUTES LATER, they were all loaded into Luke's big SUV and headed toward Denver and the mountains beyond the Mile-High City. Megan sat up front with Luke, while Cody was in back with Matt.

"Oh! I'd forgotten how majestic they are," Megan remarked at the sight of the Rockies rising abruptly behind the city. She turned to Luke. "How long till we get home?"

Home. She couldn't believe she'd let that slip. A word so personal, so possessive, so intimate. Luke must think she was a gold digger for agreeing to marrying him so readily. For even agreeing to it at all! Luke's home wasn't her home. It was just where she and Cody would live for a while, until Cody was back on the straight and narrow.

"About two hours. Matt's wife, Beth, will have everything ready for us. She's been looking after Celeste today and doing the school run with Daisy and Sash."

Megan had overheard part of Luke's cell phone conversation in the jewelry store, and to her ears, it hadn't seemed to go so well. "How do you think the girls will react to two complete strangers suddenly becoming part of the family?"

Luke glanced over at her, frowning. "I know I probably made a mess of things in my phone call, but rest assured, Beth would've found the right way to tell them."

Megan twisted her hands in her lap. "Still... Maybe Cody and I should stay somewhere else for a while, until they can come to terms with everything. It must've been a big shock for them to be told they've got a new brother *and* a new mother."

"Relax. They're good kids. They'll accept you quickly. I'm sure of it."

Megan wasn't so sure, but she guessed Luke knew his daughters better than she did. She relaxed against the seat back and closed her eyes, unable to believe how tired she was.

"WE'RE HOME." LUKE'S VOICE woke Megan. Surprised that she'd dozed off again, she opened her eyes to find they'd pulled up outside a long, ranch-style house, its lights blazing brightly in the summer evening. The sound of dogs barking and children squealing filled her ears.

Luke had climbed out of the vehicle and was opening her door. A woman came out onto the veranda and stood silhouetted in the light spilling out of the house. She ran toward the car and then Matt's huge bulk was blocking the way as he picked her up and kissed her.

"Where is she? Where is she?" Megan heard a little girl demanding and looked down to see two big blue eyes staring up at her from between Luke's legs.

Megan climbed down from the SUV. Luke stepped back a little and the child squeezed between his legs and popped up between him and Megan.

"Are you my new mommy?" she asked.

Megan was touched by both the beauty of the little

girl and the sweet innocence of her inquiry. The child reached out and stroked Megan's hand as though to check if she was for real. Megan squatted down so she could be at eye level with the child and smiled warmly. "Hi. You must be Celeste."

Celeste grinned broadly, then turned shy and twisted sideways as though seeking the protection of her father.

Megan held out her hand to Celeste and said, "I'm Megan and I'm very pleased to meet you, Celeste."

"Are you going to be my mommy?" Celeste asked again.

"Would you like that?" she asked cautiously, unsure how to approach the subject diplomatically.

"Oh, yes!" Celeste cried, and threw her arms around Megan's neck with such force it nearly knocked her backward.

Megan breathed in the sweet scent of the little girl, fresh from her bath, and felt a longing deep within her. She'd loved being a mother to Cody, but he'd stopped hugging her like that a long time ago. Megan laughed and lifted Celeste as she stood; she noticed Luke's grimace changing to a smile of relief.

"One down, two to go," he whispered to her.

She glanced around for Cody to introduce him to the girls. He was standing some distance from the group, studying another girl who was appraising him openly. She guessed that must be Sasha.

Megan took the initiative. "Celeste, I'd like you to meet my son, Cody. He's also your half brother."

"Does that mean he's only half a boy?" Celeste asked, wide-eyed.

Luke guffawed and everyone else joined in, but

Megan saw the embarrassment on the little girl's face. After all, she'd drawn what was to her a logical conclusion. She held Celeste against her and nuzzled her soft cheek. "No, sweetie, although it does sound a bit like that, doesn't it?" She waited while Celeste nodded slowly. "It means that you and Cody have the same daddy, so Cody is half a brother to you."

"Who's his other half, brother to?"

Megan couldn't help smiling. Celeste's naiveté was delightfully refreshing. "You're just too gorgeous, did you know that? And smart, too."

"Am I?"

"Uh-huh."

Celeste hugged Megan. "I love you already."

Megan kissed Celeste's cheek. Maybe meeting Luke's daughters wasn't going to be so difficult. "I love you, too," she said.

When Megan felt Luke's hand at the small of her back, urging her toward the rest of the group, she stepped away from the SUV to where another child stood waiting and watching and occasionally telling one or other of the barking dogs to, "Shut up, you idiot!"

"This is Daisy, my little lady," Luke said with a touch of irony and a smile that melted Megan's heart. There was no doubting Luke's love and affection for his daughter.

Daisy looked up at Megan, then down at her feet and back up again as though sizing her up for a coffin. "Hello," she said. Turning to Luke, the girl added, "She's kinda skinny."

"Daisy!" The three other adults reprimanded her at once.

"It's fine." Megan hastened to appease them. She

shifted Celeste to her left hip and held out her right hand. "I'm pleased to meet you, Daisy, and yes, I agree I'm too skinny. I'm hoping all this fresh country air will give me an appetite. What do you think?"

Daisy shook her hand vigorously, then nodded. "Yeah, it will. But you gotta eat your veggies, or you don't get dessert."

"Absolutely," Megan said, straight-faced. She glanced toward Sasha, who'd finally dragged herself away from staring at Cody. "And you must be Sasha."

Sasha studied Megan's outstretched hand, then accepted it reluctantly, shook it once and let go. *Okay,* thought Megan. *This one's used to being the alpha female around here.* And that was fine with Megan. She had no intention of moving in on anyone's territory.

"Cody, come and say hello to your new sisters," Megan called, and he sauntered over.

"Did your hair growed like that?" Celeste asked Cody, and reached out to touch it.

Cody pulled away. "Get lost!" he yelled. "Don't you ever shut up?"

Luke had had enough of Cody's behavior. "That's it. You!" He pointed at Cody's chest. "In there. Now!" he commanded, hitching his thumb over his shoulder and gesturing toward the barn.

Megan was relieved to see that Cody was so shocked at the anger in Luke's voice, he didn't argue or disobey. He looked around the circle of people who were all frowning at him in anger, disgust or bewilderment. Celeste had turned her face into Megan's shoulder and was sobbing softly.

Megan rubbed Celeste's back and fixed her son with a look of utter contempt. How *could* he have used such

language in front of the children and hurt such an innocent little girl? What had her son become? Tears burned
the backs of her eyes.

She'd wanted to admonish Cody but he was with
strangers and she didn't want to fracture his ego in
public. On the other hand, it wasn't acceptable that he get
away with such behavior. Thankfully, Luke had stepped
in before she'd even had a chance to open her mouth. She
watched Luke striding toward the barn, Cody behind
him, dragging his heels. At least he'd gone with Luke;
that was something. If she'd told Cody what to do, he
would've ignored her completely.

She felt Matt's hand on her shoulder. "Don't worry,
Megan. Luke's just going to talk to him, that's all."

Megan turned worried eyes to Matt. Had she really
looked as though she thought Luke would hurt her son?
Mortified, she turned back to the rest of the group. "I'm
so sorry about that. I... His behavior was unforgivable."
Celeste continued to sob quietly on her shoulder. "There,
there, sweetie. It's all right," she cooed. "Cody didn't
mean to be rude. He's just had a long day."

Celeste lifted her head. "He...he...he...*yelled* at me!"
she sobbed, and dropped her head to Megan's shoulder
again.

Megan didn't know how to placate the sobbing child.
What a way to start your life with your new family!

Matt reached over and took Celeste from Megan's
arms. She snuggled against him and stopped crying.
Matt put his arm out and drew the other woman to his
side. "Megan, this is my wife, Beth."

Beth extended her hand. "Welcome to our family,
Megan," she said, shaking Megan's hand with considerably more warmth than Sasha had displayed.

Beth was tall, blond and elegant in spite of wearing faded jeans and a camisole under an unbuttoned chambray shirt. Her face glowed with health and contentment. Megan liked her immediately. "I'm not so sure we'll be welcome after that little outburst," Megan said as she glanced worriedly toward the barn. She half expected Luke to come out pulling Cody by the ear and tell them both to get in the vehicle and send them packing back to New York.

"Nonsense!" Beth said. She reached out with her other hand and caught both of Megan's in hers. "Luke will lay down the ground rules and then everything will be fine—you'll see. He's very much the boss around here and Cody needs to know that. Come on into the house. The girls have prepared a special surprise for you."

As they mounted the few steps to the porch, Celeste wriggled out of Matt's arms and raced to open the screen door, then stood back to allow Megan to enter first.

Megan's breath caught in her throat. Strung across the hall was a banner with the words *Welcome Home, Megan and Cody.*

Everyone piled into the house after her and Celeste looked up and said, "We made it ourselves. D'you like it?"

Delighted that Celeste had apparently recovered from Cody's outburst, she smiled down at the little girl and smoothed her fair hair. "It's the prettiest thing I've ever seen, and so thoughtful." She looked around at all three girls. "Thank you. I...I'm only sorry I haven't got a present for all of you." She cursed herself for not getting them something.

"I have."

Cody stood just inside the door, Luke behind him. He no longer looked grim, so Megan presumed their "talk" had gone well.

Celeste danced up to Cody, all unpleasantness forgiven. "What've you got for me?"

Megan was curious, too. Cody hadn't purchased anything apart from clothes for himself and the PSP Matt had bought him. He unzipped his bag and took out the airline wet packs and handed one to each girl.

"Wow!" Celeste tore the cellophane wrapping off and opened the zipper. "Look! It's got a little toothbrush 'n' paste 'n' a comb 'n' a face washer 'n' mouthwash 'n' socks…." She emptied the contents onto the floor and sat down to inspect them further, then seemed to remember her manners and stood and held up her arms to hug Cody.

His face red with embarrassment, Cody bent down toward Celeste.

"Thank you, Cody. I love it!" she said, and hugged him fiercely, then let him go.

Cody stood to his full height again. "You're welcome, kid, and about before…I'm sorry."

Celeste smiled up at him. "That's okay. You prob'ly missed your afternoon nap," she told him with absolute guilelessness.

Sasha and Daisy thanked him, too, but not so exuberantly. They looked more bewildered by their strange gifts than grateful. But Megan was thankful Cody had broken the ice with his peace offering.

"I'll show you your rooms," Beth said, "and then we can have supper." She led the way upstairs and opened a door off the wide hallway. "This is your room, Cody. I thought you might like it here. It was your father's room when he was a boy."

Megan noticed Cody didn't seem too pleased by that bit of news. He sauntered inside and looked around the room, which was about four times the size of his room back in New York.

"Is there another one?" he asked of Beth.

She looked taken aback. "Well, no. Except the nursery, and I'm sure you wouldn't want to sleep there."

Megan was beginning to feel a sense of foreboding. If there weren't any other bedrooms, where was she expected to sleep? Surely not with Luke? Hadn't he assured them there was plenty of room for everyone?

Cody threw his bag onto the bed and flopped down on it. Taking that as a yes, Beth started back downstairs to a hallway leading from the living room and then to another wing of the house. She opened a door. "And these are your quarters, Megan. I hope you'll be comfortable here."

Megan went into the room, the three girls following on her heels. "This is the sitting room," Beth explained, "and here's the bedroom."

Megan walked through the pleasantly decorated sitting room, the walls covered with framed photos of dark-haired boys and young men, presumably the O'Malley boys at various stages of growth. She resisted the urge to look closer, to find the similarities between Cody and his father and uncles. She stepped gingerly through the bedroom doorway, surprised to find how plainly furnished the room was. It was neat, but there was no sign that anyone else lived there. No clothes across the end of the bed or flung over the chair, no book opened facedown on the nightstand.

Luke came up behind her and Megan felt a chill down her spine. She was supposed to share this bed with Luke?

"This is my folks' quarters," he said. "They usually live here at the ranch but they're on an Alaskan cruise at the moment. Beth thought you might be more comfortable in here…for now."

For now? Did he expect her to eventually move into his room? The thought had her heart racing and her face heating.

Beth opened another door off the bedroom. "The bathroom's through here and a closet, too. There's a kitchenette off the sitting room, so you can make your own tea or coffee if you like."

"We built this extension for my folks when I took over managing the ranch." Luke dropped Megan's bag on the bed. "But they've hardly used it. They're too busy seeing the world." As if sensing her discomfort, he said, "There's an apartment over the barn if you'd prefer. But it's not really habitable at the moment, since the plumbing's not connected."

"Oh," was all Megan could manage, immensely relieved that she didn't have to share the bed with Luke. *For now.* But what if his parents returned home unexpectedly?

"Do you want to freshen up or have supper?" Beth asked.

Megan observed the way Matt was looking down at his wife. *Oh, to have the love of a man like that!* she thought.

"I'll just wash my hands if that's okay. I'm sure the girls need to get to bed."

Celeste said, "We've had dinner, 'cause I have to be

in bed at seven-thirty. But Aunt Beth said we can stay up a bit later, 'cause tonight's special."

Megan smiled at the little girl who was now her step-daughter. She was adorable. The fact that this child had never really known a mother's love broke her heart.

Luke had explained during the drive that Tory had deserted the girls before Celeste's first birthday. She'd taken off with a rodeo star, leaving the girls with him. Having met them, Megan was even more bewildered as to why Tory would throw all this away for the itinerant life of a rodeo star's lover.

Megan vowed then and there that she'd more than make it up to Celeste, and Daisy and Sasha, too, if they'd let her.

"Come on, girls," Beth said. "I think I can hear my little Sarah waking up."

Forgetting completely about Megan, Celeste dashed out of the room and down the hallway, followed by her sisters.

SUPPER CONSISTED OF A BEEF casserole with mashed potatoes and peas. The girls, who'd already eaten dinner, had a dessert of ice cream and fresh fruit salad.

"I'm sorry it wasn't something a little more spectacular for your first night," Beth apologized. "But this is the girls' favorite meal and they felt you'd like it, too."

Megan smiled at them. "It's the most delicious beef casserole I've ever tasted. What's the secret?"

Daisy piped up. "Black Angus, the best beef in the world."

Megan was surprised by the pride in the girl's voice and by her knowledge. "You seem to know a lot about the cattle," she said, and ate another mouthful.

"Daisy's going to take over the ranch from Daddy one day," Sasha told her. It was the first time she'd addressed Megan directly since they'd sat down. And Megan got the distinct impression she was warning Megan about *who* exactly was going to inherit the ranch!

"Oh, you don't have any interest in it?" Megan asked her.

"Hell, no!"

"Sasha! Penalty box," Luke snapped.

The girl's face fell. "Oh, come on! I haven't had any allowance for weeks because of that penalty box. Darn it."

"And you won't have any for the next few weeks if you keep that up, young lady," Luke said from the head of the table.

Sasha ignored her father and spoke to Megan. "I don't like dumb old cattle. I'm going to marry a man with a stud farm in Kentucky."

"In your dreams!" Daisy taunted from across the table.

Sasha narrowed her eyes. "Better than hearing silly old cows mooing all night and stepping in their poop all the time!"

"Sasha, penalty box!"

"Yeah, like horses don't poop," Daisy reminded her, completely ignoring the fact that her sister had just been fined for cussing. "What're you going to do? Get your husband to put diapers on them?"

Celeste giggled at that, then so did Cody. Soon the whole table was in uproar as Matt lifted a napkin in the air and pretended he was diapering a horse.

The rest of the meal passed companionably, but when Megan yawned, Beth took that as their cue to leave. "I'm sure you've all had a long day, so we'll get going," she said, standing. "Girls, could you help me clear the table and load the dishwasher, please?"

"Let me." Megan got up, but Matt laid a restraining hand on her arm as he stood to help his wife. "You'll be busy enough tomorrow with four children to look after instead of one. I imagine that's going to be quite a shock to your system. And a husband, too." He glanced at Luke, and Megan saw the look that passed between the two brothers.

Megan swallowed hard at that reminder of her new responsibilities. *A husband, too.* And *four* children. In one day, the size of her family had tripled, which would take some getting used to. Well, starting tomorrow she'd do just that—get used to it. For the moment, all she wanted to do was sleep.

"Will you read me a bedtime story?" Celeste stood beside Megan's chair and slipped her little hand into Megan's.

"Yes, of course." Megan stifled another yawn, not sure if she'd last to the end of the story. "But first, I'd better see everyone off."

"Don't worry about us," Matt said. "We'll be back tomorrow. The rest of the family's coming over for a barbecue and can't wait to meet you both." He walked to Cody's seat and held out his hand. "Nice to have you in the family, Cody."

Cody shook Matt's hand, surprising Megan. She mused that Matt sure had a way with kids. Normally, Cody would've ignored such a polite gesture and turned away.

Beth came from the kitchen. "All cleared up. Ready,

darling?" she asked, and Matt went to collect their baby daughter from the nursery.

"I'll have to wait for my chance to hold her until tomorrow," Megan said wistfully as she gazed at the sleeping baby.

Beth laughed. "You'll have to stand in line. She's everyone's favorite toy around here."

"She has been for six months, darling." Matt gazed down at his wife and daughter with loving eyes.

Celeste tugged at Megan's hand and drew her toward the stairs, reminding her of the bedtime story. "Bye, everyone," Megan called. "It was so nice to meet you, Beth, Matt. See you tomo—" Her last words were cut off as she was dragged down the hallway by Celeste, impatient to get to her room.

Megan tried not to yawn too much while Celeste brushed her teeth. Then she sat on the side of the small bed and opened the book the child handed her. Celeste leaned over and gave Megan a big hug and kiss. "Just'n case I fall asleep before you finish," she said, then laid down and closed her eyes.

Megan began to read, making an effort not to yawn too often. She watched Celeste's chest rise and fall rhythmically and continued reading, yawning after every few words, not taking in one little bit of the familiar story.

Hans Christian Andersen's *The Little Mermaid* had been one of her favorites as a little girl. Night after night, she'd pester her nanny to read it to her.

But all she could comprehend right now was that it was a fish out of water story—in more ways than one. Exactly how Megan was feeling.

Chapter Three

"D'you think she's dead?"

"No, dummy. See? Her chest's goin' up 'n' down."

"She looks kinda dead." Megan opened an eye to find Celeste leaning over her. "Oh! You're alive. That's good. D'you wanna come and play with my dolls?"

Megan opened both eyes. Celeste and Daisy were right beside her bed. Sasha stood behind them, her arms crossed, wearing a stern expression. "Do you want coffee?" she demanded in a voice that said what she thought of people who slept half the day away.

Megan nodded. She rubbed her eyes and glanced at the bedside clock. Ten-thirty! Good heavens. Today was the first day of being a mom to four kids and she hadn't even been up in time to get their breakfast. The aroma of strong coffee filled the room. Sasha stood at the end of the bed, now with a tray in her hands. She placed it on Megan's nightstand.

"Daddy made you coffee early, but you weren't awake so he made you some more. You *still* weren't awake. I made this one," she said, and Megan could hear the exasperation in her voice.

Well, that's telling me, Megan thought. Luke had been in twice with coffee expecting her to be up and then Sasha had felt she needed to make some. Hoo, boy. What a way to start married life. She sat up and took a sip and tried not to sputter. It was strong enough to strip paint.

"I did it the way Daddy likes it," Sasha explained. "You like it black with no sugar, don't you?"

Actually, Megan liked it with cream and one sugar, but she wasn't going to upset Sasha any more than she apparently already had. She forced down another sip and shook her head when the caffeine kicked in, clearing the fog in her brain instantaneously. "Mmm, this is good," she managed to say around the cotton-wool feeling in her mouth, and looked down at herself. She was dressed only in her camisole and panties. She quickly pulled the covers up, wondering, *How did I end up here, undressed and without my bra?* She tried to remember how she gotten from Celeste's room to hers last night, but drew a blank.

She smiled at Celeste and Daisy, who were watching her intently. Sasha had left the room. "Did you sleep well, girls?"

Celeste climbed onto the bed. "Not as well as you. We been waitin' *ages* for you to wake up and be our mommy."

Megan smiled again. At least Celeste and Daisy seemed pleased she was here; she couldn't say the same for Sasha, though. The girl's disapproval was palpable.

I must've slept so long because of the country air, Megan told herself. She'd never slept till ten-thirty since her college days, and only if she'd pulled an all-nighter studying for exams. "Did I finish your story last night, Celeste?"

Daisy answered that one. "Nope, you fell asleep on her bed and Daddy had to carry you here. You were snoring."

Megan's face heated. Luke must've undressed her, too!

She ventured another sip of the extrastrong coffee and then Sasha returned bearing a second tray, this one loaded with crisp bacon and toasted bagels. The aroma had Megan's mouth watering. She'd barely eaten a thing at dinner, she'd been so tired. But now that the coffee had kicked in, along with the fresh country air, her appetite had, too.

Sasha set the tray on her lap and stood as though waiting for Megan's acknowledgment.

"Thank you, Sasha. This looks lovely, but you really didn't have to. I could've gotten up and fixed myself breakfast."

Celeste helped herself to a piece of bacon and crunched down on it. "Sasha does the cooking on the weekends, when Mrs. Robertson isn't here. That's what she gets her allowance for."

"Who's Mrs. Robertson?" Megan asked. Luke hadn't mentioned anyone else living here, too.

Daisy grabbed some bacon. "She's our housekeeper. When Grandma isn't here, she comes in and takes care of us during the week. She cleans the house and fixes our dinner 'cause Daddy doesn't have time. I get my allowance for helpin' with the animals," she added.

Megan looked at Celeste. "And do you get an allowance, sweetie?"

"Uh-huh, but not very much," she said with a heartfelt sigh.

Megan grinned. Celeste was so easy to love. "Well,

now that I'm here, you don't have to do any more of those chores, Sasha." Megan addressed the older girl, who, unlike her sisters, hadn't taken up residence on the bed.

But instead of welcoming Megan's offer, Sasha's features became shuttered. "That's been my job since Mom left. I like doing it."

Megan didn't care for the idea of such a young girl being tied to the house, but on the other hand, realized she'd better tread carefully about taking over any responsibilities Sasha felt were hers. "All right," she said slowly. "Please let me know if you'd like any help."

"I don't need any help. I can cook and sew and clean." Sasha was sounding downright belligerent. The last thing Megan wanted was to get off on the wrong foot with her eldest "daughter." Getting along with Celeste was a breeze and Daisy seemed to be pretty easygoing, but breaking down the protective wall Sasha had erected was going to be a problem. Megan wished she'd paid more attention when Luke was talking about the girls. That might've given her greater insight into their characters—particularly Sasha's. The first chance she got, Megan was going to have a long talk with Luke and get a few things straight regarding her duties and the girls'.

"Will you do my hair?" Celeste asked.

Megan studied the little girl's attempts to braid her hair. It stuck out all over the place. She smiled. This was something she *could* do. "Sure, sweetie."

"Mine, too?" Daisy asked.

Megan looked at Daisy's wild mop of dark curls and didn't think there was much that could be done. "You've got beautiful curly hair, Daisy," she said. "What could you possibly want done with it?"

Daisy brushed it out of her eyes impatiently. "It gets in the way when I'm ridin' or tyin' calves. I wanna have it cut really short, but Daddy won't let me."

"I can see why. Most girls would kill to have hair like yours." Megan reached out and combed her fingers through it. "It's so soft, too."

Daisy made a disgusted noise and left the room, saying, "I gotta go help one of the hands teach Cody to ride. He's already fallen off of Killer 'bout a dozen times."

"Killer!" Megan's body was drenched with fear. "You've got a horse called Killer and you let Cody on it!" she almost screeched.

Daisy crossed her arms and leaned against the doorjamb. "Relax. Killer's about as old as our uncle Adam, 'cept Uncle Adam's got more teeth," she said with a grin. "Cody's such a klutz he just can't stay on. Hasn't he ever been around a horse before?"

The only horses Cody had ever seen were the ones that drew carriages around Central Park. "Er, no, he hasn't," she confessed. "Do you think it's wise for him to learn to ride so soon?" She appealed to Daisy, who seemed to know everything there was to know on this topic.

"We live on a ranch. If he doesn't learn to ride, he's gonna to have to walk. We've got over five thousand acres." With that, Daisy turned and marched out the door.

Megan bit her lip. She'd assumed Cody was still in bed, too. Daisy didn't seem concerned about Cody's learning to ride on a horse called Killer, so maybe that was okay. Deciding she should get up and look around the place, get the lay of the land, Megan threw back the covers and put her feet on the floor. "If you'll excuse me, girls, I'll take a shower and then join you in a few minutes and we can see about your hair, Celeste." She looked at Sasha. "I could do something with your hair, too, if you like."

Sasha's expression became shuttered again. "I'm not a baby. I can do my own hair," she said curtly, and picked up the tray.

Oh, dear! I've done it again, thought Megan. "Thank you for the coffee and breakfast, Sasha. It was all delicious." Megan didn't think the odd white lie would go amiss if she was going to be practicing diplomacy.

THE SHOWER WAS GLORIOUS, with plenty of hot water and a strong spray—the total opposite of the often icy dribbles that emitted from the shower back at her tiny apartment in New York.

Megan made the most of it, shampooing her hair and then conditioning it. She thought again about how she'd gotten to bed last night and felt hot all over. Not only had Luke removed her cotton pants and matching jacket and top, he'd also removed her bra, leaving her to sleep in her camisole and panties. She rinsed the conditioner out of her hair.

Maybe Luke had carried her to her room and Beth had stayed to undress her? Yes, that sounded more plausible. More appropriate, anyway. She didn't know how to broach the subject with Luke to find out if that was the case.

When she stepped out of the shower, a foggy full-length image of herself stared back from the mirror.

She wiped it with her towel, bent over and wrapped the towel around her head, turban fashion, then straightened and looked at herself. Daisy was right—she *was* too skinny. The worry of the past few months, since Cody had gotten mixed up with the wrong crowd, had taken its toll on her health.

Because she'd had to fill in the hours she'd missed at work, either while trying to track down where he was or going to court with him, her appetite and eating patterns had been chaotic. Now her arms were too skinny, her hip bones stuck out and her legs looked twice as long as they usually did. She thought about Luke's hands on her breasts last night as he removed her bra—then picked up another towel and wrapped it around herself. She definitely had to find out who'd taken off her clothes, if only to stop her hormones kicking in at the thought of Luke—her *husband*—touching her in places she hadn't been touched, *he* hadn't touched, for many, many years.

Megan hurried to her bedroom and burrowed into the shopping bag, coming up with fresh underwear and a pair of jeans and chambray shirt. Luke had assured her the outfit was appropriate for the ranch. Until she saw what everyone else was wearing, and her clothes arrived from New York, it would have to do. In the meantime, she'd better get her only other set of clothes into the washing machine. Hadn't Beth said everyone was coming over for a barbecue tonight—or had she dreamed that?

"There you are!" Celeste said with relief in her voice when Megan stepped into the kitchen. "I thought you mighta gone back to sleep!"

Megan held up her brush, a mirror and some hairpins,

clothes under one arm. "I was just seeing what I had to fix your hair," she explained, then looked at Sasha. "Do you mind if I do some laundry, Sasha? I'll need clean clothes for tonight."

Sasha looked her up and down. "What you've got on will be fine." She pointed at Megan's bare feet. "'Course you'll need some shoes. I got some riding boots that might fit you. What size do you take?"

Megan didn't see how a twelve-year-old could have size seven-and-a-half feet but she told her, anyway.

"I take an eight, so you can have an old pair of mine." She held out her arms for the laundry. "I'll go throw these in and then I'll get my boots."

Megan held on to the clothes when Sasha tried to take them from her and then relented. It wasn't worth wrestling with the kid over a load of wash. If that was the way she wanted to play it, then fine. For now... "That's very kind of you, Sasha," she said. "Thanks for both the boots and doing the wash. Is there anything I can help with in return?"

Sasha squared her shoulders and disappeared from the room without answering her. Megan stared after her, bewildered.

"Don't worry about *her*." Celeste gestured at her sister's back. "She's almost a *teenager!*" She climbed up on the table and sat cross-legged among a heap of glossy fashion magazines opened at various pages. "See these hairdos? Which one will work for me?"

Megan glanced at the sophisticated models with very complicated dos and didn't think any of them would suit her—at least, not for another twenty years. But she pretended to give the photos a great deal of consideration.

"Hmm. Well, you know, of course, that all of these will need hot rollers and gallons of hair spray."

Celeste's face fell. "I don't have none of that stuff."

Megan lifted her brush to run it through Celeste's hair. "Will you trust me enough to do something special?"

Celeste gazed at her with excitement in her eyes. "Uh-huh." She nodded and lifted a mirror to admire herself. "Will I look as pretty as them?"

The little girl was as feminine as her older sister Daisy was a tomboy. "Oh, I guarantee you'll look a lot prettier than them," she assured her. She set to work brushing the tangles from Celeste's blond tresses. "You've got such pretty hair," she complimented the child. "It's like spun gold."

"Grampa says it's the same color as Grandma's when they were younger. 'Course, hers is kinda gray now, since she's so old."

They kept up a friendly chatter through the hairdressing session, Megan curbing the urge to curse when the French braid she was trying to create didn't seem to be working out the way she wanted. Still, she hadn't tried to do one since college, so it was no wonder her fingers were a little rusty.

Celeste sat through the ministrations, constantly moving her head from side to side and asking, "Is it ready yet? I wanna see!"

"Not yet, sweetie." Megan chewed on her lip as she braided the strands of hair.

"That's okay," Celeste told her. "I like this."

LUKE STOOD JUST OUTSIDE the screen door to the back porch, watching Megan working on Celeste's hair. They were a picture of female contentment, although perhaps

Megan—alternately chewing her lip or sticking out her tongue in concentration—didn't seem quite as contented as Celeste. If there'd been any doubts in his mind as to whether he'd done the right thing in marrying Megan so impulsively, they were dispelled as he stood there, battered Stetson in hand, watching his youngest child being mothered and fussed over.

He remembered carrying Megan to her room last night, enjoying the feel of her in his arms, her soft sigh as he placed her on the bed. He'd removed her shoes and lifted her feet onto the bed, but since nights got cold in the mountains, even in midsummer, he couldn't leave her lying on top of the comforter. He eased it from under her and was about to cover her when he realized she probably wouldn't be comfortable sleeping in tight pants.

So he'd slipped them off her, swallowing at the feel of her bare skin beneath his fingers. He'd quickly covered her lower half. But then the jacket she wore might tangle around her during the night, waking her, so he sat her up and gently drew her arms from the sleeves.

She'd moaned slightly, stretching her neck. It probably wouldn't hurt to loosen her bra, as well.

He'd rested Megan against his shoulder and felt underneath the back of her camisole top. As he unfastened the clasp he told himself he was going to stop right there. But then she seemed tangled in the bra straps so he pulled them down her arms, then slid her bra out from under her top.

He'd swallowed again as he looked at the tiny scrap of fabric in his hands. This probably wasn't right, undressing a woman without her consent. But it was too late to undo what he'd done. And she *was* his wife. Not a stranger.

Gently, he lowered Megan to the bed, pulled up the covers and tiptoed out of the room.

As he watched his youngest daughter and his wife now, Luke knew that Celeste and Megan would be just fine. Daisy, too. Sasha was another matter. His eldest daughter had told him in no uncertain terms that she wasn't going to be calling Megan "Mom."

"I'm sure she doesn't expect you to, Sash," he'd said.

"As long as she knows I already have a mom and I don't need another one coming in here and taking over."

Luke had been baffled by her reaction. Since Tory had effectively stopped being a mother to Sash years ago—making only the occasional phone call, sometimes even forgetting her birthday—Luke wondered why she was vehement. Furthermore, he'd thought Sasha would welcome not having to shoulder so much of the responsibility she'd taken on when Tory had left.

On the plane journey back to Denver, he'd convinced himself that the timing of Megan's advent into their lives was perfect. Now Sasha would have a chance to be a carefree teenager. Maybe it'd take a little time, but he was sure she'd come around once she realized all the fun she'd be missing. Still, he'd better warn Megan before she started moving in on Sasha's "territory."

"THERE!" MEGAN SAID with relief as she finished the French braid.

Celeste turned her head this way and that. "I can't

see!" she protested. Megan picked up the other mirror and held it behind Celeste's head.

"Ooh! That's so pretty," she cried, and moved her head from side to side again, admiring it from all angles. Then she spotted her father standing on the back porch. "Look, Daddy! Mommy's made me look so pretty!" She jumped down off the table and went to throw herself into her father's waiting arms.

Mommy! She called me "Mommy"! Megan thought, her heart soaring.

Luke lifted Celeste into his arms and settled her on his hip. "You sure are pretty." He turned and smiled at Megan, filling her with a sense of unreasonable joy. She'd wanted to stay mad at this man, but it was impossible. All he had to do was smile and she was like a lump of putty in his hands, ready to be molded to his whim.

"You've got a fan here. But don't be surprised if she demands to have her hair done like this every day now," he said.

Megan raised one shoulder. "That's okay. I need the practice." She smiled shyly at Luke and wondered if she should ask him now about putting her to bed last night. Feeling her face warm with embarrassment, she decided to put the question aside for the moment. She cleared her throat. "Daisy tells me that Cody's learning to ride."

Luke put Celeste down and she ran out to find someone to show her hair to. He hung his hat on a peg near the door, walked to the refrigerator and grabbed a bottle of water. He turned back to her after taking a long swig. "Do you have a problem with that?"

Megan could read the challenge in his eyes. She had a problem with a lot of things, not least the fact that twenty-four hours ago she was a single mother living in New York City with her son. And today she was a married woman living in the middle of the Colorado Rockies with her son, three stepdaughters and a husband she barely knew.

Cody's learning to ride on a horse named Killer was a small matter by comparison. If Megan was honest with herself, she'd admit that she was secretly pleased he'd fallen off a few times and each time had gotten back up on the horse. It showed he hadn't quit. Cody's tendency to give up easily when the going got tough was something else that had worried her about his behavior this past year. He used to be so tenacious, so determined to finish anything he started, but lately, he'd found it easier just to shrug and claim things were "dumb."

Megan believed in taking risks, believed it was a way to personal growth and fulfillment. But she'd had to take so many in her thirty-five years that she would rather not have taken—like being a single mom. But despite her beliefs, despite Cody's supervision, she couldn't help worrying about his safety.

She leaned against the edge of the kitchen counter. "No, I don't have a problem with that. If you think he's safe, then I trust your judgment." Hard as that was to say, she meant it.

Luke gave a tiny nod, as though pleased with her reaction, then headed for the door.

"Luke…" He stopped and turned slowly toward her. "I…I think…that is…when you have some free time that…you and I need to talk."

He nodded. "After lunch we can take a ride over to

the meadows by the creek. We'll have plenty of privacy there."

We'll have plenty of privacy there. Was that a threat— or a promise?

Chapter Four

"I've arranged to meet my bank manager in town so we can get you a credit card," Luke said, and glanced at his watch. "We'd better get going. The bank closes at noon."

Megan shrugged, embarrassed at feeling like a kept woman. "Luke, I can't take your money."

"You're my wife. How do you think you're going to pay for groceries if you don't have a credit card?"

"Aren't the banks almost closed by now?" she said, trying to stall him. She didn't want to get into the financial side of their relationship yet.

Luke faced Megan and took her hands, forcing her to look at him. "He's staying late as a favor to me. I want to get this done today, Megan. It can't wait until next week. So stop making excuses to avoid it."

Feeling as if she'd been backed into a corner, she tried to make one more stand. "I have a debit card. I don't need a credit card. It's too easy to get into debt with one."

"If you want to keep your debit card, then that's fine. But we need to put money into your account. My bank manager can facilitate that."

"Okay," she conceded grudgingly. "I'll just freshen

up." She turned to leave, hating to release Luke, but needing to get away from him. When he got up close like that, acting protective, it did things to her insides. Things she didn't want to examine. Not now.

"And while we're there, we'll get you a credit card."

Megan spun back, ready to deny she needed or wanted one, but Luke was already going out the screen door.

She hurried to her room, determined not to keep him waiting long.

As LUKE HELD THE DOOR OPEN so Megan could precede him inside the bank, a man walked out.

"Gil," Luke said. "How are you?" They shook hands.

"Fine, Luke. And you?" His curious gaze encompassed Megan.

Luke drew her toward him and said, "You might not have heard the news, Gil, but I got married yesterday. This is my wife, Megan."

Gil smiled and offered his hand to Megan. "Congratulations and I'm pleased to meet you."

"Gil McIntyre is an old friend and the ranch accountant," Luke explained. "He keeps me on the straight and narrow. Doesn't let me get carried away with buying too much stock." He grinned. "I mean horses and cattle, not stocks and shares."

Megan smiled dutifully. She found it odd that an accountant would presume to tell a rancher how to run his business, but since she knew so little about ranching so far, she didn't inquire.

Several other people came out of the bank, and Luke and Gil moved aside to let them pass, continuing their conversation.

Luke checked his watch. "I think this stampede means they're about to close, so we should get moving. I want Megan to meet Joe Hickey and have him set up a credit card for her."

Gil frowned and looked at Megan. "You don't ha—"

"Like I said, we'd better go," Luke cut in. He pressed his hand against the small of Megan's back, indicating she should go ahead.

Megan turned to say goodbye to Gil.

"It was nice to meet you," she said.

"You, too," Gil said with a smile. "You must come over sometime and meet my wife, Betsy."

"Don't get too friendly with her, Gil," Luke said in a joking voice. "I might have to fire you soon. Megan's studying accounting and when she's qualified, I may just have her look after the ranch finances."

Gil's expression didn't change, but Megan sensed a wariness. *Was* he worried about losing this job?

"You know you can't fire me, Luke. Remember who found that error your previous CPA made in the accounts? And don't forget the huge refund you got from the IRS when I filed that amended return."

Megan felt that although Gil's words sounded teasing, there was a mild threat beneath the surface.

Luke didn't seem to notice anything awry. He laughed, clapped Gil on the back and said, "See you around, buddy. Say hi to Betsy for me."

Inside the bank, Megan couldn't shake her feeling abut Gil.

"Why did you cut him off earlier?" she asked.

"Because he was going to ask you why you don't have a credit card and that's none of his business."

"But he's your accountant!"

"And you're my wife, not part of the fiscal structure of the ranch. Our business as husband and wife is ours alone."

Although Luke's words were delivered a little harshly, Megan experienced an incredible feeling of being protected, safeguarded by Luke.

Against her own wishes, Megan was starting to fall in love with Luke all over again.

WHEN THEY ARRIVED BACK at the house, Luke nodded toward the corral. "Want to come and see how Cody's doing?"

"Okay, I'll just tidy up here and see if Sasha needs any help."

"About Sash. Can you go easy on her? She's used to making a lot of the decisions around the house, so I'd appreciate it if you'd give her some space."

Megan didn't like his suggestion that she'd given Sasha a hard time. That was the *last* thing she wanted to do. And for heaven's sake, the child was only twelve. Why did he allow a youngster to assume so much responsibility?

"I've worked that out already. Thank you," she said coolly and, after collecting her things, left the kitchen.

LUKE WATCHED HER GO, her back held straight. *Women!* First Sasha snapped at him and now Megan. *Hell.* He was only trying to help her get along with her new stepdaughter. He walked out, letting the door slam behind him. Who was he kidding? His son had barely exchanged three words with him this morning. Three words that weren't cussing of one kind or another.

Cody hadn't been happy about being dragged off to the barn last night, but there were a few ground rules around the ranch and Luke wasn't prepared to cut Cody any slack where they were concerned. He'd seen Megan plead with her son to behave, seen how fearful she was of his reaction. Well, that was going to stop. Cody was going to be *told* and expected to *obey*—starting with the number-one rule. No cussing around the children and no cussing in the house.

He'd told Cody that he could cuss all he liked out in the paddock or the barn, provided he'd checked to make sure there weren't any women or children around. He didn't really like the idea of Cody using bad language at all, but figured the kid had to have some outlet for his frustrations. If he came down too hard on him and forbade all swearing, the kid was likely to ignore him altogether.

The second thing he'd pointed out was that Cody was part of the family now. That meant he had sisters to consider, not just himself, and he wasn't to hurt them in any way.

Cody had looked puzzled. "I never hit anyone!" he protested.

Luke had put a hand on his shoulder. "I didn't say you did—or would. I mean that you hurt Celeste's feelings. She's a sweet kid who's never had a mom or a brother and she was very excited about meeting you. You didn't have to snap at her like that."

Cody had stuck out his bottom lip. "Yeah, well, I never had a sister before, either—or three of 'em—and

I don't like how nosy girls are and how they talk all the time."

"Get used to it, son." He liked the way the word sounded, even if he wasn't too enamored of his son right now. "Other O'Malley men have managed to adapt to having women in their lives. They're not too bad—once you get used to 'em." He'd jerked his head toward the others. "Let's go back and get something to eat."

The mention of food had Cody's legs moving in long strides—typical of the O'Malley men.

Since last night, though, Cody had studiously ignored him in a battle of wills. At least the kid had gotten back up on Killer the first time he'd fallen off. Luke had been watching one of the ranch hands teach Cody to ride. The kid had been about to give up and storm back inside, but then he'd spotted Luke and climbed back on.

Luke had smiled to himself and stayed around to watch some more. Daisy and Brian, the ranch hand, were patient with Cody, encouraging him and coaching him on how to stay in the saddle. After he'd watched Cody nearly fall off a few more times, he walked away. By then Cody was more hooked on learning to ride than competing with his father.

LUNCH CONSISTED OF LEFTOVER casserole on toast. Sasha had insisted on setting the table and reheating the casserole herself. She'd allowed Megan to make the toast.

"This is Daddy's favorite Saturday lunch," she told Megan in a tone that implied she'd better not mess up the toast.

"Sounds like your dad likes home-style cooking. What do you like to cook, Sasha?"

"Anything Daddy likes to eat."

Megan thought that was a strange response. Didn't Sasha want to cook things *she* liked to eat?

"What are we supposed to prepare for the barbecue tonight?"

"I'm defrosting steaks. And Uncle Will is bringing ribs. You don't need to bother with anything."

Megan had had just about enough. It was clear the girl resented her being there. Well, tough! Because Megan wasn't going anywhere. Particularly after she'd seen the smile on Cody's face when he'd called to her across the yard to show her how he could sit on the horse and even stay on when it cantered around the corral. Megan had climbed onto the rail fence and watched him ride Killer, and then Daisy had mounted a huge horse and opened the gate to the yard. Killer had trotted out—with Cody on his back—into the open fields!

What if Cody panicked? What if the horse took off? Daisy had slapped Killer's rump and Killer took off at a slow canter. Cody held on, tossing his head back. His laughter came to her as they disappeared from sight.

"I'd *like* to bother, if you don't mind, Sasha," she said now. "I'd like to make some sort of contribution to this evening—to feel that Cody and I are part of your family."

"You don't have to. Everyone's bringing something so you don't need to do anything."

Sasha was determined to shut her out, her resentment palpable. Megan couldn't wait until she and Luke took that ride. She might suggest he have a long talk with Sasha—in the barn, if necessary!

She decided to change the subject. "How many people will be coming?"

Sasha picked up a knife and waved it in the air. Megan resisted the urge to duck. "Let's see," she said. "There's four of us and two of you and Uncle Matt, Aunt Beth and Sarah. Uncle Jack and Uncle Will and Aunt Becky and their two kids. Uncle Adam *isn't* coming so that makes…"

"Fourteen," Megan said. "Counting the *six* of us."

Sasha shot her a glare.

Megan pretended she hadn't noticed. "Why won't your uncle Adam be coming?"

"He lives in Boulder. He keeps to himself."

"Sounds mysterious. What does he do for a living?" Megan was aware there were five brothers, but back when she'd known Luke, Adam had been in junior high.

Sasha was putting on a pan of water to boil and got out a packet of rice. Megan knew it couldn't be for lunch so assumed she was making it for tonight. "He's a firefighter."

"And he's not married?"

"No. Why? Are you interested?"

Megan was taken aback. "Interested in Adam?"

"Yeah." Sasha turned toward her challengingly.

"Sasha, I'm married to your father. Of course, I'm not *interested* in his brother."

"You could get it annulled. You haven't slept together yet—except to have Cody. Uncle Adam's awful good-look—"

"Sasha!"

Luke's raised voice from behind the screen door shocked Sasha so badly she dropped the knife. It landed point down in the linoleum between Megan's feet.

Luke practically tore the door off its hinges as he

marched into the kitchen and stood over his daughter. "Apologize to Megan at once for that comment," he demanded.

"Why should I? You don't even know if he's your kid! I heard you telling Uncle Matt!" she cried.

Megan felt her blood chill. Luke didn't believe Cody was his? And he'd gone ahead and *married* her?

"That was before I went to New York, young lady!" he thundered. "Now, apologize to Megan!"

Megan held up her hands, trying to placate him. "Really, Luke, it doesn't matt—"

Luke cut her off. "It does to me." He turned on Sasha. "I won't stand for it, young lady. Do you hear me?" he roared. But Sasha, equally implacable, scowled at him, making no move to obey.

"There is no doubt in my mind that Cody *is* my son and consequently *your* brother, so get used to it. Fast! And Megan *is* my wife, whether *you* think this is a *real* marriage or not."

Megan wanted to cheer at his words. It felt so good to have someone standing up for her and her son. But on the other hand, Megan knew Sasha was hurting. She wanted to fold the girl in her arms, tell her everything would be all right.

"Then why aren't you sharing a bedroom?" Sasha was apparently unfazed by her father's rebuke. "People who are *really* married sleep together—or hadn't you noticed that?"

"And people who aren't married sleep together, too!" Luke ran his hand through his hair and got his voice under control. "The reason Megan and I don't share my bedroom is none of your business, Sash. And it's certainly none of your business to go suggesting she might want to run out on me—*us,*" he corrected, "and marry Uncle Adam."

"How do I know you're really married, then?" Sasha asked stubbornly. "Except for that dumb old ring you gave her, and that doesn't prove you're married. You should've asked if it was okay with us!" Tears filled Sasha's eyes.

Megan's heart went out to the girl, who believed her father had betrayed them by not asking their approval first. She placed a hand on Sasha's shoulder but the girl shrugged it off. "Do you really mind that much, Sasha?"

Sasha whirled to face her. "'Course I do! I don't want you coming in here and trying to be my mother, telling me what to do, taking over!" She turned back to her father. "You shouldn't have brought them here! It's going to ruin everything!"

Luke caught her heaving shoulders in his hands and pulled her against him. "It's okay, sweetie," he murmured. "I married Megan because it was the right thing to do. Cody needs a father. I wasn't trying to replace your mom with Megan."

Megan was aghast. What was he saying? That he wanted to be a father to Cody but didn't want her being a mom to his daughters? They'd *definitely* better have a long talk after lunch! She slipped out of the kitchen unnoticed and went to her room.

If she'd had anything to pack, she probably would've packed it right there, grabbed Cody and then gotten as far from the ranch as possible. She didn't need this. Didn't need the teenage tantrums and the rejection and bad attitude. The *hell* with Luke and his need to play daddy. The *hell* with Cody demanding they get married.

The *hell* with all of it! First thing Monday morning, she was going to see about an annulment because she wanted out! "Dammit!" she cried, picked up a pillow and threw it across the room.

"You gotta pay the penalty box," a tiny voice said from behind her.

Megan spun around to find Celeste regarding her seriously, sweet little face puckered in a frown.

Her heart melted. If nothing else, this dear little girl needed her. Forget everything else. If she could make a success of being a mother to Celeste, then that would be enough for Megan. The rest of them would just have to live with it. She wasn't going anywhere or getting any annulment, because Celeste needed her—and she needed Celeste.

Megan opened her arms and Celeste ran into them. She picked her up and cuddled her, loving her little-girl smell mixed with horse and something sweet and sticky that she was smearing on Megan's cheeks as she kissed her.

"I love you," Celeste said, and hugged Megan tight.

"I love you, too, sweetie." Megan hugged her right back and wiped at her tears.

A polite cough from the door had Megan looking up to find Luke standing there. Sasha stood behind him.

He strode toward them. "She really does love you, you know."

"And I really love her, too," Megan said, then glanced at the door.

Sasha stood there trying to look belligerent, her arms crossed as she lounged against the jamb.

"Sasha's come to apologize," Luke said. "Come in, Sash."

"Luke, please, this isn't necessary." Megan could guess how humiliated Sasha felt being forced to apologize for her behavior. She knew Luke meant well but it would only serve to make things more difficult between the two of them.

Sasha sauntered into the room in much the same way Megan had seen Cody walk when his pride had been shattered. "You can make some dessert if you want," she said.

Megan thought it was a strange apology but wasn't going to point that out.

Celeste clapped her hands. "Oh, goody, we can make trifle!" She squealed and wriggled out of Megan's arms. "Come on, Mommy, I'll help you," she said, grabbing Megan by the hand and trying to drag her out of the room.

"Sasha!" Luke's voice warned again.

Megan broke in before Luke had a chance to say anything else. "Thank you, Sasha. I'd like that very much." Ignoring Luke's warning growl, she let Celeste pull her out of the room.

"You gotta boil the water for the Jell-O first," Celeste was telling her as she got up on the table. "I'm not allowed to do that, so you'll have to. Then I can help you make the cake, but you'll have to open the cans of fruit." She got down off the table again and went to select some canned fruit from the pantry.

Megan laughed. "Okay, Miss Bossy, I'll boil the water. But I've never heard of Jell-O in a trifle before."

"It's *Irish* trifle," she explained patiently. "Handed down through generations of O'Malleys."

Megan smiled. "That sounds like something you've heard often."

Celeste rolled her eyes. "Uh-huh."

"Then I guess you'd better get me some Jell-O mix."

"Oh, yeah." Celeste got down and chose several different flavors from the pantry. "We can make lots of colors, 'cause there's lots of us."

Megan filled the kettle, and while they waited for it to boil, they opened several packets of Jell-O and placed the contents in bowls. "We'll let it cool while we're having lunch," Megan said. "Then we can make the sponge cake. How about putting those cans in the fridge so they can chill during the afternoon?"

Megan poured the boiling water into each of the bowls and stirred the Jell-O to dissolve, then moved them to a bench to cool before putting them in the refrigerator.

Luke lounged against the kitchen doorway, his arms crossed, watching them. "You two work well together," he observed, then walked to stir the Jell-O for something to do with his hands while he formulated what to say to Megan, "I'm sorry about Sasha," he said quietly. "It's going to take her a while to adapt."

Megan picked Celeste up. "Can we talk about this later?" She indicated over her shoulder that Daisy and Cody were coming up the steps of the back porch.

"Later," Luke said, and Megan wondered if his voice didn't hold a note of promise.

Chapter Five

"You sit a horse well," Luke said as they rode out into the meadows beyond the house.

They'd just given the horses their heads for a brisk half-mile canter and had reined them in to a walking pace.

Luke breathed in the air of the beautiful June day. His spirits always lifted on days like these and Luke hoped it would have the same effect on Megan.

"I had lessons when I was a child. Every Saturday morning at Miss Dustin's Riding School."

"Sounds upmarket."

Megan pulled a face. "It was. Can we talk about something else?"

Interesting. She didn't want to talk about her own childhood, yet she was a natural with kids. She'd sure wound her way into Celeste's heart. They'd made the sponge cake together and put it in the oven and Megan had left Celeste in charge of keeping an eye on the timer. Then, when the cake was done, Celeste was to get Sasha to take it out of the oven. Luke had warned Sasha that if there was the slightest hint the cake had been sabotaged, she was in big trouble.

"I'd prefer it if you let Sasha and me work things out

between us." Megan's words broke into his thoughts and he pulled his horse, a huge bay gelding, up beside her mount, an old palomino mare called Sage.

"Whoa there, Rocket." He soothed the horse when it wanted to go racing toward the meadows near the creek where the sweetest grass grew. Megan turned in the saddle to face him. "I think your little outburst in the kitchen earlier today only made things more difficult. Sasha's been humiliated in front of the person she despises most. It's not going to be easy to reach out to her now."

"She has no right to despise you," he argued. "You haven't done anything wrong."

"In her eyes, I've hurt her by coming here, pretty much unannounced, and taking her place as head female in the house. Had I known what I was walking into or had time to think about it, I wouldn't have married you quite so readily."

Her forthright statement had him stopping his horse. "You didn't have any choice," he reminded her. "It was either get married or let Cody go to juvenile detention."

She turned Sage to draw level with him. "I'm not so sure he would've carried through on that threat."

"And *I* wasn't prepared to take that chance. He's my son and I'll do *anything* to save him from juvenile detention. We're married now, whether we like it or not."

Megan clicked at Sage and the two horses fell into step walking side by side again. "The circumstances are unpalatable to me, too, but seriously, have you thought about what happens next? How we're going to manage a marriage where the kids know we don't share the same room—let alone the same bed? That'll get around school awfully quick. People will start to talk."

Luke shrugged. "So let 'em. Our marriage is nobody's business but ours. We got married to give Cody the stable family life he needs. When we succeed at that, then we'll move on."

Needing to get away from Megan—being close to her made him want her too much—and to clear his head, Luke kicked Rocket into a gallop and took off across the paddock.

MEGAN WATCHED HIM GO, a chill invading her heart where love should have resided. *Then we'll move on.* Move on to what? Other partners, but stay married? She needed to keep reminding herself that theirs was nothing more than a marriage of convenience, created to save their son from juvenile detention. She shivered in spite of the warm June afternoon, then clicked her tongue at Sage, urging the mare to an easy canter, taking pleasure in the fresh air and solitude—two things in very short supply in her part of New York.

The meadow she rode through was rich with wildflowers and the sky seemed to stretch on forever.

LUKE DISMOUNTED and slapped his horse's rump to indicate he could trot off and eat his fill, then helped Megan down, turning her to face him.

Resting his hands on her hips, he looked into her eyes as if trying to read what was there, then lowered his head to kiss her.

Startled, she pulled back. "Luke!"

He smiled slowly at her. "Just getting the wedding kiss I missed out on yesterday."

Megan flushed as she remembered how the judge had pronounced them husband and wife and told Luke he could kiss his bride. He'd bent to place a hurried kiss on Megan's cheek. It had missed and ended up somewhere near her ear, probably because she'd turned her head away. She cursed herself for being so angry with Luke that she'd fumbled the opportunity to feel his warm lips on hers.

Luke moved his hands farther around her back and pulled her closer, so they were touching from knee to waist. "We're married," he reminded her hoarsely. "Married people are allowed to kiss each other, you know."

Setting her hands on his chest, she left them there for just a moment, savoring the feel of his hard muscles beneath her fingertips, then gently, reluctantly, pushed him away.

"We need to talk, Luke. Isn't that why you brought me here?" she asked. She walked toward an outcropping of boulders by the creek and sat down. Picking a daisy, she examined it, then threw it in the water and wondered if Luke had brought his wife here. Had this been a special place for them? It was a beautiful spot; the wide, crystal-clear creek bubbled over submerged rocks and tiny wildflowers grew along its banks.

He hunkered down in front of her. "Okay, let's talk. Why didn't you tell me about Cody?"

Although Megan had been expecting the question, it didn't mean she was prepared for it. She lifted her shoulders. "It's a long story."

"I've got—" he glanced at his watch "—'bout four hours."

Megan forced a smile. "Let's just say I didn't think you'd be interested in hearing from some girl you'd had a short affair with during spring break, telling you she was pregnant with your child." At his look of disbelief, she said, "Remember, we hadn't even exchanged addresses or phone numbers. I was pretty sure that as far as you were concerned, our relationship ended the day I left Spruce Lake. I assumed you'd forgotten me by the end of the week."

"You didn't keep our date."

She bit her lip. When they should've been on their date, Megan was crying her eyes out at the airport as she waited for a standby flight back East. Away from Luke and his betrayal.

"I...I wasn't well."

"You could've called the restaurant. I was there for over two hours, looking like a fool, telling people they couldn't have my table because I was waiting for my date. My date who didn't show up."

I didn't show up because I'd learned the truth about you that afternoon, in the locker room at the rec center. You were engaged to Tory. I heard her talking to another girl, bragging about the big wedding you were going to have. About the baby you were having!

Megan wanted to scream the words at him. But saying them wouldn't change anything. She'd discovered it was better to leave the past in the past.

She sighed. "Let's drop it, okay? The reasons don't matter anymore."

"Don't tell me it doesn't matter!" He stood and paced. "I had a *right* to know I was going to be a father..." He halted and fixed her with a glare. "Unless you weren't sure who the father was."

That hurt. That *really* hurt. How dared he, of all

people, accuse her of sleeping around when he'd already got another girl pregnant!

"I was sure," she said through icy lips. Angered, she jumped to her feet and paced away from him, then spun around. "You knew I was a virgin!"

He didn't even have the grace to flinch. "Then why didn't you try to contact me?"

"I did!"

Silence descended on the glen. Even the creek seemed to have stopped its babbling.

Finally, Luke crossed his arms in a confrontational stance and said, "If I'd heard anything from you, I would've acted on it."

"I sent you a letter from the hospital, the day I gave birth to Cody," Megan said, trying not to let her voice waver. Even all these years later, the feelings of rejection, from both her parents and the father of her baby, hit her hard.

She didn't want to think about her parents right now. It brought up too many bad memories of how she'd always been made to feel second best. Both of Megan's parents had unabashedly favored her older brother. There was nothing Jordan could do wrong in their eyes. He was an A-student, a gifted sportsman, a golden boy. When Jordan had expressed an interest in following in his father's footsteps and studying law, he'd been given a brand-new imported sports car.

Megan hadn't particularly cared about that, but it was yet another example of how Jordan was always rewarded, while she was always criticized. Getting pregnant in her junior year of college had sealed her fate. Her feelings of rejection and being not quite good enough were brought into stark relief. She'd hoped that her brother would stand by her. But Jordan proved to be as fickle as she'd suspected and had cut her completely out of his life.

"I didn't get it," Luke said, waking Megan from her musings. He stood with arms crossed. Challenging her.

He didn't believe her, and Megan didn't believe him. She shook her head and turned away. Why, oh, why did she give in to Cody's demands and agree to marry Luke? Neither of them trusted the other and she didn't see how they ever would.

"Don't hide from me, Megan. And don't lie to me."

She spun back to him, more angry than she'd ever been in her life. She felt the fury in her stomach, her chest, her heart. She rushed at him and beat his chest with clenched fists.

"How dare you, you bastard! How dare you accuse me of lying! I wrote you a letter, and a month later I called the ranch! I did everything I could to contact you." The words and the anger spilled out of her as she hit him again and again as if it could purge fifteen years of wretchedness from her soul.

"Your *wife* answered the phone!" she screamed.

Luke had remained steadfast, taking her blows, but now he gripped her forearms, preventing her fists from striking him.

"*What* did you say?"

"You heard me!"

"I wasn't married when we were dating," he said in a slow, measured voice, as if it was important she understand that.

Megan wrenched her arms out of his grasp. "You were

married when I called. The baby was *my* responsibility. There was no point in taking the matter any further."

She steeled herself against the knowledge that Luke had made love to her when he was already engaged to someone else. *Don't you know how cheap that made me feel?* she wanted to shout.

"It takes two people to make a baby, or at least it did the last time I checked. Your pregnancy was my responsibility, too."

"No, it was mine. Alone." At Luke's puzzled look, she explained. "Remember when you'd run out of condoms and I assured you it was a safe time of the month for me?"

Luke nodded. "I remember," he said hoarsely. He'd been so crazy for her, he hadn't wanted to delay, hadn't wanted to go out and buy more condoms.

"Turns out it wasn't a safe time, after all. It was my mistake and I paid for it."

Looking at Megan now, her shoulders slumped in defeat, her once-sparkling eyes filled with dull pain, he found it hard to reconcile her with the person he'd known back then.

He had to take some of the blame for the change in her. It couldn't have been easy raising a child on her own. She'd come from a wealthy, privileged family, been a junior at Wellesley when he'd met her, yet there was no sign of affluence in the outfit she'd worn yesterday. Gone were the designer labels she'd once sported. And her Rolex watch. Had she sold it to make ends meet? The guilt of realizing how bad things had been for her weighed heavily on him.

Wanting to keep Cody away from his old neighborhood, he'd been relieved when she consented not to return to her apartment to collect anything and instead agreed to have their possessions shipped to Colorado. They'd used the few hours before their flight to shop. Megan had done so carefully, paying a frugal amount for her jeans and shirt in the department store.

He'd produced his credit card and insisted she buy whatever she wanted, but Megan had shaken her head in firm denial, paid for her clothes out of her well-worn wallet and gone off to buy a few toiletries. At least he'd managed to talk her into letting him pay for Cody's things—by pointing out she'd been supporting their son for fourteen years and now it was his turn. Cody hadn't had a problem with it, choosing name brands and stocking up on the latest gear for teens. Megan had stood back and let him go ahead, but she hadn't been happy about it—not one bit.

He'd wondered about that, too. Was she upset about the amount being spent? That she couldn't afford it and he could? Or was it something else? A fear that Cody would change his allegiance from her to him simply because he could buy their son the things she couldn't? That he would therefore buy Cody's love? Teens could be such fickle creatures and he could understand why Megan felt that way. Well, she could relax on that score, because Cody despised him as much today as he had yesterday.

"What about your folks?"

Her snort of derision said more than words.

"I take it they weren't pleased to learn you'd brought back a souvenir from spring break?"

She dragged her eyes up to his. "They weren't. And they were downright unpleasant when I refused to have an abortion or put the baby up for adoption. They washed their hands of me when I wouldn't tell them who the father was, so they could go after you with a shotgun."

He picked up a stone and rubbed it between his fingers, then let it fall. "Why didn't you tell them? Why didn't you chase me down as soon as you knew? I would've done the right thing by you."

The right thing? Megan wanted to lash out at him. *Oh, sure!* She wanted to cry. *As if you would've broken off your engagement to marry some lovesick idiot who happened to be pregnant with your child!*

Instead, she kept her emotions in check and said quietly, "We would've gotten married for all the wrong reasons. It wouldn't have lasted."

"I don't consider giving a child two parents and a family who loves him the wrong reasons for getting married. Tell me this. Why did you agree to marry me yesterday but you didn't want to marry me fifteen years ago?

"You know why I agreed yesterday! I had no *choice*. It was either marry you—or lose Cody!"

"What made you think you could do it on your own?"

She shrugged. "Stupid arrogant pride, I guess. I was young. I thought anything was possible. And I was out to prove something to my parents."

"You took a chance on my son's life to *prove* something to your parents?"

She whirled around. "What are you implying? Cody's *life* was never in danger! Yes, I had to quit school, but fortunately I got a job working on the financial section of a Greenwich newspaper that provided on-site daycare."

"Since you dropped out of college by the time you had him, it couldn't have paid too well."

"It didn't. But it was the only job I could get where I could have a baby at work with me. I managed. I managed for twelve years until the newspaper closed down and then I had to take two jobs because Cody needed health care and it costs a lot to feed and clothe a teenager. And we had to keep finding new apartments because whenever I fell behind in the rent the landlord suggested there were other ways I could *pay the rent!*" She choked out the words, angry with Luke for pushing her so hard.

Curbing her anger, she said, "The same way some of the other desperate single moms 'paid the rent.' No way was I going to let *that* happen. I was trying to finish my degree one course at a time, but I'd lost interest in economics, so I switched to a more practical option. Everything I did, I did for Cody and I always worked around his schedule, his needs. Or...I tried to."

She hated the catch in her voice, but she was powerless to stop it. Luke was implying that she was a bad mother, that she'd taken unnecessary risks. Didn't he understand? She'd had no choice! "I couldn't do what my parents demanded." Her thinly held control broke and she covered her face with her hands and wept softly. "I couldn't kill our child," she whispered.

SHOCKED BY HER ADMISSION of how hard her life had been, Luke felt guilty that he couldn't have made her life and Cody's easier for them. Megan might not have wanted marriage, but he still could've supported them financially. He rubbed her back in soothing strokes. He was aware there were things she wasn't telling him, but for now, he'd let it go. She needed reassurance, not reprimands.

"You did a great job, Megan, in spite of everything. You should be proud. He's a good kid."

Megan looked up at him, her eyes brimming with pain. "A good kid who nearly ended up in juvenile detention."

"Thanks to you and a smart, caring judge, he didn't. And he never will," he said with conviction. He released her and moved away, feeling uncomfortable with their contact. At first it had been to comfort her, but now that Megan had recovered her composure, her closeness was doing other things to him—things Luke didn't want her noticing.

"Thank you," she murmured, and he turned back to her, surprised by her remark. "Thank you for believing the judge...for believing enough to take a chance on coming to New York."

Her voice was thready, and her lip trembled. Her emotions were naked, laid bare. Luke wanted to hold her, but resisted the urge. What Megan needed more than that, he thought again, was the reassurance that she'd done the best thing for Cody.

"No. I'm the one who should be thanking *you* for not succumbing to your parents' demands to get rid of him. That must've taken so much courage." He took her right hand in his, raised it and splayed their fingers, a symbol of togetherness.

"I'm not that noble. They convinced me to keep an appointment at the abortion clinic, but when I went there..." She took a heaving breath. "When I stood outside those doors and thought about what would happen to my baby in there—I couldn't cross that threshold." She released his hand, her shoulders slumped in defeat.

Luke placed two fingers beneath her chin, raising it so she had to look into his eyes. He needed her to know how he felt. Needed her to know she was no longer alone. "You *are* noble. And courageous and beautiful and the best mom Cody could have." He leaned forward and dropped a gentle kiss, on one cheek and then the other.

Her eyes held uncertainty mixed with wonder. "Do you *really* mean that?"

"Yes. And now that I've seen you with Celeste, I couldn't imagine anyone else being a mother to her, either."

Megan smiled, the first genuinely happy smile she'd given him. "She's just so sweet. I adore her already."

"And she adores you."

"I'm working on Daisy, but she's always on the go and doesn't seem to spend much time inside."

Luke couldn't help laughing. "She likes you a lot. She told me just after lunch."

Megan's eyes brightened. "I like her, too. She's completely fearless."

"She thinks you need fattening up," he said, and Megan laughed, too.

"I got off on the wrong foot with Sasha, though."

"Partly due to my interference and partly due to her pigheadedness. I won't interfere any more between you," he promised. "I figure you'll both have to shake things up and see how they settle. She's a good kid, generous to a fault."

"She is. She didn't hesitate to lend me a pair of boots and she likes to help out around the house."

Luke nodded. "I wish she wouldn't do so much, but it's something she's always done since Tory left, in spite of the housekeeper coming in during the week and Mom being here most of the time."

There was a silence. Then Megan asked, "You said she's only twelve?"

"Uh-huh."

"How long after I went home did you and…Tory get married?"

Luke frowned. "Why do you want to know?"

"I thought—since it produced three beautiful daughters—your marriage must have meant a lot to you."

Luke turned away and stared out at the stream. "Tory and I got married about a month after you left town."

Megan's heart contracted with pain at hearing that. "I see. So why would you have offered to marry me if you were already engaged to someone else at the time?" *Why did you sleep with me when you were practically a married man?*

Luke picked up a stone and tossed it into the creek, watching it skip across the water. Finally, he said, "Tory and I had been dating for a few months. I told you we'd split up a couple of weeks before I met you, and it was the truth. She was…too possessive."

Megan watched him, not commenting.

"When I finally got it through my thick head that you weren't interested in me," he went on, "I got roaring drunk one night, ended up sleeping with her and she got pregnant."

His explanation didn't match Tory's revelations to her friend in the locker room at the rec center. Something wasn't right. "If she got pregnant just a little later than me, then where's the child?"

Luke's face twisted bitterly. "She claimed she had a miscarriage. It happened a few weeks after we were married."

"I'm sorry," Megan said softly, and touched his arm.

Luke liked it when she touched him. It made him feel wanted. He'd honored his marriage vows, tried to love her, but Tory had thrown him aside, along with their daughters. It had taken him years to realize Tory was never pregnant, had faked the miscarriage. She'd taunted him with that during one of their many arguments.

"But you have three lovely daughters. I hope that's eased your pain."

Luke looked at her and managed a smile. How different would it have been for him if he hadn't been so stupid, hadn't let Tory trick him into marrying her? But he still wouldn't have known about Cody—and he wouldn't have had the girls. His marriage had been a living hell—parts of it—but his three daughters were the result. They'd made it worth suffering through the bad times.

"Luke, I can't pretend it's going to be easy making this marriage work, but I'm willing to give it my best shot—for the sake of the children. I…I'll understand if you need to seek the company of other women. All I ask is that you please not bring them home."

Luke stared at her, incredulous. "*What?* Just what are you saying?"

"I'm saying that I'll make the best of this marriage and that I'll look the other way if you need…female companionship outside of our marriage."

Luke shook his head to clear it. He couldn't be hearing her right. "Why would I want to do that?"

"Let's be honest, Luke. This is nothing more than a marriage of convenience between two people who barely know each other."

"But—"

"You made it pretty obvious last night that you don't want me sharing your bed. You put me in another room at the other end of the house."

Luke was dumbstruck. He'd put her at the other end of the house for three good reasons. He'd assumed she'd want nothing to do with him. She was exhausted. And she'd be out of temptation's way—although he'd spent tortured hours staring at the ceiling for most of the night.

He shook his head. "You've changed so much. You seem so unsure of yourself, Megan. Where has the carefree young woman of fifteen years ago gone?"

"I had to leave her behind a long time ago."

"Why? Because you had a child?"

"Not only that. To…survive."

They were both silent for a moment. Then she said, "I don't expect you to find me desirable anymore. That's why I won't stop you from looking elsewhere for… companionship."

He recalled Cody's implication that there'd been a variety of men in and out of his life. Was that why she believed it was okay? Was that why her expectations were so low and she seemed so defeated?

He wanted to yell at her, shake her, drag her into his arms to elicit some sort of response from her, try and dredge up some vestige of the person she'd been.

"You think I want another woman in my bed?" he demanded. "You think I'd break my vows? You think I'm that shallow?"

He hated the way she stood there, her silence confirming every word he spoke. Why would she think so little of him? Hadn't he tried to prove his commitment to her and Cody by marrying her? Yes, it might have been prompted by concern for his son, but he'd *never* treat her with such flagrant disrespect, such disregard.

At a loss to understand why they were so brittle, so distant with each other. "Touch me," he whispered. And waited. Hoping to find the bridge to her heart.

MEGAN SWALLOWED. There was nothing in the world she wanted more. So what held her back? For fifteen years, she'd longed to feel Luke's arms around her, know his kisses again, the way he made love so tenderly.

He was so close, she could lose herself in his masculine smell. She breathed in the scent of horse and hay and...Luke.

She lowered her eyes and let them rest on his mouth, then his strong neck, his wide shoulders, his broad chest. He was bigger than she remembered, more filled out, even more desirable now than he was all those years ago. She ached to have him wrap his arms around her, feel his lips on hers.

Megan dredged up every ounce of resistance she could muster to protect herself from Luke. She could never let him know she'd loved him all that time, wept with wanting to feel him hold her again. But she'd spent too many of those years suppressing that yearning; she couldn't allow it to crumble so easily, couldn't let down her defenses and confess the truth: that she'd loved him then and still loved him now.

"Touch me," he said again. But this time it sounded more like a plea than a command.

All she had to do was lift her hands to his chest....

She glanced back up into his eyes, saw the naked hunger in their depths

With a tiny intake of breath, she understood that his longing was as great as hers.

She raised her hands and placed them on his chest. He felt so good, so strong, beneath her fingers, she wanted to coil them into his skin, lay her face against his chest, breathe him in.

Warmth and sheer male strength emanated from him, emboldening her as she gazed into his eyes, daring him to take the next step. But he didn't. If anything, the hunger she saw there had deepened, become more raw.

It took all her willpower not to pull his head close to hers, to slip her arms around him and hold him so tightly the breath would be forced from their lungs. She wanted his lips at her throat, his mouth on her breasts, his tongue...

She molded her hands to his chest, wanting him, *needing* him, so much. But Luke was letting her lead this dance. If she wanted to, she could walk away. She knew by his stance that he was giving her that choice.

She ran her hands up his chest, to his throat and around to the back of his neck, clasping them behind his head. She was on sensory overload by now, powerless to resist him.

"Kiss me," he murmured, and she leaned into him, bringing her lips to his, needing the contact, longing for it, reveling in it.

"Kiss me the way you've wanted to be kissed all these years," he whispered.

And she did, realizing that Luke, too, must have

dreamed of her kisses as she'd dreamed of his. He wrapped his arms around her so tightly, she gasped for air. He eased his hold a little, giving her space to breathe, and angled his mouth over hers. His kiss was at first demanding, then softened with tenderness.

His arousal pressed hotly against her belly.

With a tiny whimper of surrender, she gave him everything.

THEY LAY IN EACH OTHER'S arms, feeling satiated, complete.

Megan rolled away from Luke to stare up at the sky through the branches of the tree overhanging the creek. Tears of happiness ran from the corners of her eyes and she wiped them away, not wanting Luke to know how much their making love had affected her.

The word *profound* sprang to mind and she smiled secretly. No, it had been more than that, so much more intense. Had he hoped they'd make love when they headed out on their ride? He'd brought birth control. Surely that was a sign that he wanted them to share a bed, start living like a real husband and wife.

She rolled back toward Luke and placed a kiss on his chest.

We're going to make it! she wanted to call into the meadow. Wanted to let every living creature within earshot hear her rejoice.

Luke lifted her so she lay on top of him. He held her face in both hands and kissed her. "Thank you," he breathed against her mouth.

She smiled and said, "I was thinking of saying the same thing to you."

He kissed the tip of her nose and said, "Maybe

now you'll realize you don't need a succession of men through your bed to keep you happy."

Megan froze. What was Luke saying? That he believed he hadn't been the only man she'd made love with these past fifteen years? She was too choked up, too shocked, to say anything that would dispel the notion. The unmitigated *nerve* that he could think that of her! She bit down hard on her lip and forced the tears not to flow, forced her breathing to slow. How *dared* he condemn her for something she hadn't done!

For fifteen years, she'd kept her feelings for Luke to herself. Kept the love in her heart a secret. Kept herself away from the potential hurt of another relationship. And here she was, in the middle of Colorado, right back where she'd started.

PUZZLED BY HER SILENCE and the sudden stiffness in her posture, Luke drew back to look into Megan's eyes. He saw nothing but loathing in her gaze. And unshed tears.

Megan leaped to her feet before he could grab her arms. She reached for her clothes and put them on, her hands fumbling with the buttons of her shirt. She gave up and tied the ends beneath her breasts. "How dare you treat me like a common whore," she whispered through clenched teeth, leaving Luke so stunned he didn't know how to react.

After pulling on her jeans, Megan caught Sage's bridle and swung up onto her horse. Without a backward glance, she turned the mare's head and rode out of the meadow.

Chapter Six

Luke clambered to his feet and strode to where Rocket grazed. He rested his head against the horse's flanks, wondering why Megan had lit out of there so fast, said the things she had.

The only conclusion he could come up with was that she regretted their lovemaking.

She didn't want him. Not as her husband. Not as her lover. Theirs was a marriage of convenience. How could he have forgotten that so soon?

If Luke hadn't been expecting guests tonight—guests to celebrate his *marriage*—he would've gone down to Rusty's Bar. Instead, he had to get himself under control and ride back home and pretend he had a marriage that was going to work *for the sake of his children*. Certainly not for him.

He glanced up at the never-ending Colorado sky and tried to push away the memories at the edge of his subconscious—Tory turning up that night and relating to him what she'd overheard Megan saying in the change rooms at the rec center. "She was laughing at you, Luke. Saying she'd never laid a hayseed before, that the girls back at college would think it was hysterical that she'd seduced you and then kept you waiting. She wanted to see if she could fool you because you were just a lovesick country boy."

Dammit! He swung up into the saddle and grimaced against the pain. Damn Tory! Damn Megan! Damn every blasted woman he'd ever met!

He'd believed Tory when she'd told him that. He'd known her since they were kids. Why *wouldn't* he believe her?

Tory had known about Megan, since she'd bumped into them at Rusty's one night. She'd been pleasant to Megan, leading Luke to assume she'd gotten over their breakup.

A couple of days after Megan had left, he'd run into Tory again, and she'd told him what she'd overheard. That had been such a low point, he'd drunk too much and let Tory take him home to bed. In the morning she'd informed him she was several weeks pregnant.

She said she didn't want an abortion, and Luke didn't feel right about it, anyway, so he'd done the only thing he could. He'd married her. He didn't love Tory, but when she'd miscarried, he'd been devastated. Over the next couple of years, doubts had started to surface, cracks had appeared in the marriage and he'd been on the point of asking for a divorce when Tory had gotten pregnant— this time for real. He'd stayed.

He'd stayed for three years and then when he couldn't stand it anymore and wanted out, she'd gotten pregnant again. The third time she'd been just as desperate to hang on to him, but as was Tory's nature, once Celeste was born, she'd lost interest in her marriage and children. She rarely spent a night at home, preferring to trawl every nightspot in the county.

They had blazing fights and, during one of them,

Tory confessed that she'd never been pregnant and her miscarriage was a fake. Luke had already guessed, so he hadn't reacted and that had only enraged her more.

When she met a rodeo star at a local bar, Tory claimed she needed more excitement in her life, so she'd packed her bags and left without even saying goodbye to her girls. Luke let her go.

He'd felt nothing for Tory by the end. Her obsession with him and other men had hurt too many people. He'd suspected Tory's crazy obsession with him had kept him and Megan apart all those years ago, but how could he prove it? She'd lied so convincingly it was hard to separate fact and fiction.

MEGAN MADE IT BACK to the ranch and her bedroom, barely maintaining her composure. It was only when she'd closed the door to her room and stepped under the shower spray that she allowed her pent-up emotions free rein. Humiliated by Luke's accusation and angry for succumbing yet again to his lovemaking, she wanted to rail against the world.

LUKE RODE BACK to the ranch cursing himself.

He'd thought he and Megan had a chance of making this work. He grimaced as he remembered the way she'd fumbled with the buttons and instead tied that scrap of fabric beneath her breasts and gotten up on Sage and galloped off as if she couldn't get away from him fast enough.

"What's bitin' your butt?" Daisy asked when he rode up to the corral fence. He leaped off Rocket's back, threw the reins over the railing and strode toward the house.

Luke turned. "Watch it, young lady," he warned, in no mood for smart remarks. "Or the penalty box is going to be overflowing this week."

Daisy liked hanging on to her money, so he knew she'd apologize.

"Sorry, Daddy. But Megan rode in here lookin' really bad a while ago and now you're comin' from the same direction."

Luke could see the hurt and confusion in Daisy's eyes. He walked back to her and ruffled her hair. "Sorry, squirt. It was wrong of me to take my temper out on you—or Rocket," he said, observing the gelding's heaving sides. He'd crossed over the creek and ridden the horse hard into the foothills behind the meadow to check on his brood mares and their foals. From there he could see the ranch house in the far distance. His haven, his home.

Apart from his family, it was the only solid thing he could rely on in his life.

"S'okay," she said, and shrugged out of his embrace.

"Can you give Rocket a brush-down, honey? I'll pay the penalty box for you."

Daisy brightened and said, "Sure."

Luke bent and gave her nose a peck. Of all his children, Daisy was by far the most independent and least demonstrative. Well, at least until Cody showed up.

"I've been thinking I should increase your allowance. You do more than your fair share around here."

Daisy's eyes widened. "Really?"

"Yep, really. And I might backdate it to the beginning of the year."

That promise got the desired response as Daisy

threw her arms around his waist. "I love you, Daddy," she said.

"And I love you, squirt," he said, hugging her back.

He knew he wasn't demonstrative enough with his kids. He didn't mean to be so distant, never imagined he'd be such a hard taskmaster as a father. Life had sent him down a path he wasn't happy about traveling, but it wasn't fair of him to take it out on his daughters.

His throat closed as Daisy continued to hug him. He coughed to clear it, then gently pried her away.

"I've got to go talk to Megan," he said. "Can we discuss your raise a bit later?"

Smiling, Daisy shrugged. "Sure." She picked up a brush and started to groom Rocket.

He mounted the rear veranda steps, eased his boots off and opened the back door. Sasha and Celeste were in the kitchen cutting up cake.

Sasha looked up guiltily. "I was only trying to help Megan, Daddy. I'm not taking over," she explained. "She seemed upset, so I thought she wasn't well. Celeste and I are finishing the trifle for her."

Luke hadn't realized how stormy he must've looked himself until he'd seen the worry reflected in Sasha's eyes. "It's okay." He patted her shoulder reassuringly. "That was kind of you. I'll go talk to her."

"Me, too!" Celeste piped up, climbing down from her stool.

Luke scooped her up and put her back on it. "No, darlin', Sash needs your help here. I'll be back in a jiffy." He turned and strode out of the kitchen, through the living room and down the hallway. He paused outside Megan's door and rapped lightly. When there was no response, he turned the handle and stepped inside.

He could hear a shower running in the bathroom and walked to her bedroom. He paused outside the door and listened, then walked in.

Above the sound of running water he could hear Megan crying.

Unable to comfort her, fearing she'd lash out at him for intruding, he made himself take a step backward. And then another and another. Silently, he left her room.

Back in his own bathroom, he turned the faucet on cold, and stepped under the punishing spray. *You heartless bastard!* he cursed himself. *She's done nothing other than come here and try to help you to provide a normal family life for our son. And now look what you've done!* Luke had no idea exactly *what* he'd done wrong, but he planned to find out, once Megan had regained her composure.

WHEN MEGAN HAD COLLECTED herself enough to face their guests, she got out of the shower and dried off, then splashed cold water on her face, hoping that would subdue the swelling around her eyes. The outfit she'd arrived in yesterday, freshly laundered and pressed, hung on the outside of her closet door. Her underwear, also freshly laundered, was on the end of her bed, neatly folded.

There wasn't a hair dryer in evidence so Megan brushed her hair and pulled it into a ponytail. Dressed in her clean clothes, she took a deep breath and headed to the kitchen. She'd been short with Sasha and Celeste, who'd greeted her warmly when she'd come inside a half hour ago and headed straight to her room. She needed to make it up to them.

"I dunno," she heard Celeste saying, "I don't think Mommy's going to be happy that we're makin' the trifle."

"Too bad," Sasha snapped. "It's gotta get chilled enough for tonight."

Megan entered the kitchen and forced a bright smile. Celeste sat on the kitchen counter looking so serious, Megan's heart went out to her. She'd called her "Mommy" again. How wonderful and *wanted* that word made her feel.

No longer needing to force her smile, she said, "Sasha's right, sweetie, the trifle does need to chill." She lifted Celeste off the counter and shifted her onto one hip, then turned to Sasha. "Thank you for thinking of that. I'm afraid I've been indulging myself in the shower too long."

Sasha merely nodded and continued pouring the custard over the trifle. "I made custard, too. You forgot to do that before you went riding. It had to chill, as well."

Megan couldn't understand this girl, who was so generous, yet wanted to push Megan away, usually with veiled accusations. "Thank you," she said, not wanting to inflame the situation. "I guess I just assumed there'd be some in the refrigerator."

"This isn't New York City. We live on a ranch. We don't rely on buying everything from the supermarket."

Duly chastised, Megan said, "You're right, of course. I'll have to get used to that, won't I?" she agreed, and moved Celeste to the other hip. She was a bit too old to be carried around, but Megan loved having her chubby little arms around her neck, squeezing perhaps a little too tightly.

"How about if I put you down here," she said. "We don't want my outfit too crushed before the guests arrive." She sat her on the kitchen table and started to unwind the French braid in Celeste's hair, which was coming out. "Thank you, Sasha, for ironing my outfit. How do you get the creases so neat and crisp?"

"Spray-on starch."

And lots of it, Megan thought, noting the stiffness of her collar rubbing against her neck. So there were clearly some things it was okay to get at the supermarket. She turned her attention back to Celeste. "Hold still, sweetie, and I'll redo your hair, so it's nice and pretty when everyone gets here."

"I need a bath first. You can wash my hair, too."

"Sure. Let's do that, but since I can hear Daisy running water upstairs, you can have your bath downstairs, okay?" She turned and let Celeste climb onto her back. "Will you be okay here, Sasha, or would you like me to help with anything?"

"I don't need your help," she said.

Have it your way, miss! And while you're at it, get that chip off your shoulder, Megan thought, then nearly bumped into Luke as she piggybacked Celeste out of the kitchen.

Luke caught her arm as she stepped back. The warmth of his touch sent desire licking through her body as she remembered the way he'd touched her as they made love in the meadow. She rejected that memory, determined this man would never get to her again.

"Can we talk?" he asked, his dark eyes pleading.

Surprised by the pain and intensity she saw in his expression, she said, "I'm going to give Celeste her bath."

"Now, please. It's important."

Megan bent to let Celeste slide off her back, saying, "Why don't you go get undressed and I'll start your bath?"

"Okay, Mommy." Celeste danced off toward the hallway. Moments later they could hear her clattering up the stairs to her room.

"Don't get in the bath until I'm there!" Megan called.

"Okay, Mommy!"

Megan smiled at Celeste's retreating back. She'd never get tired of hearing Celeste call her "Mommy."

She followed Luke to the downstairs bathroom. He put in the plug and set the bathwater running, then gripped Megan's hand and drew her down the hallway to her room.

Once inside, he locked the door and turned to her. "I want to apologize for my behavior this afternoon. I know you came here with the best intentions for our son's welfare. I appreciate that you're trying your hardest with my girls. I don't expect, and neither will I ask, anything more of you. I want to assure you that I won't be seeking the company of women outside our marriage and that...I won't trouble you for any more...marital favors, either." With that, he reached to unlock the door, but Megan stayed his hand.

"Just a minute," she said. "I've listened to you. Now you can listen to me."

Expressionless, he nodded.

"You took something very important away from me when you said those hurtful words about other men in my life." She drew in a deep breath. "That hurt so badly,

Luke. You destroyed something in me that I've fought very hard for."

He stared at her blankly, then asked, "You mean you're not mad at me for making love to you?"

"No. I'm angry at myself for letting that happen so soon. I'm upset with you for that comment afterward."

"But—"

"I didn't have much self-esteem left after what I'd been through trying to raise our son on my own, but what little I had, I held very dear. I had *never*—would *never*—succumb to allowing a man to share my bed in order to get by. When you said that, it made me realize you neither respected me nor had any real understanding of how difficult it's been to raise our son on my own."

"But—"

"You should've known there was no one before you. And there's been no one since. Yet you were prepared to believe the worst of me, to humiliate me by insinuating those things."

Luke shook his head. "I'm sorry," he said. "I thought that was what Cody meant back in the judge's chambers. I thought it was the reason he wanted us to get married, so there'd be some stability in his life. Obviously, I misunderstood what he'd said."

"That sort of thing *did* go on in our neighborhood. But you misinterpreted what he said and applied it to me and that hurts so much."

Luke took both her hands in his. "I'm sorry from the bottom of my heart. I'd never intentionally hurt you, Megan."

He halted as though waiting for her to speak, and when she didn't he said, "We've let too many misunderstandings keep us apart for the past fifteen years. Can we try to put them aside and start fresh?"

"I'd like that," Megan managed to say. But deep down she wondered if the time to start fresh had expired too long ago.

"Mommy! The water's goin' over the sides!" Celeste's plaintive call brought them both back to the present.

Megan reached around Luke, unlocked the door and opened it. "Coming, sweetie," she called, then slipped past Luke and headed to the bathroom.

Chapter Seven

Twenty minutes later, Megan felt almost as wet as Celeste. She lifted the child from the bath, set her on the mat, looked down at her damp clothes and thought glumly that Sasha wouldn't be happy to see how she'd treated her handiwork. They hung limply from her body. Her top and blouse hadn't fared much better, but as she didn't have anything else to wear, they'd have to air dry. At least she still had her jeans.

"Can you be a big girl and finish drying yourself while I go put on some dry pants?" she asked Celeste, then reached in to pull out the plug.

"Okay…but hurry, Mommy."

Megan placed a kiss on Celeste's forehead and slipped out of the bathroom. Sasha was waiting in the hallway with her arms crossed. She looked Megan up and down with disdain.

"I…I got wet," Megan stammered, wondering why she allowed this child to get her so flustered and feeling guilty.

"You can't wear them tonight even if I do get them dry," Sasha said, disapproval dripping from every word.

Megan kept her temper in check. "You said my jeans

would be fine for this party, didn't you? And my top and blouse will dry quickly enough."

"Everyone'll be here any minute," Sasha told her. "You can borrow my hair dryer."

Touched again by Sasha's strange but basically generous ways, she followed the girl upstairs to her room. "This is a lovely room, Sasha," she remarked, admiring the professional finish. "I like the contrast of the orange and purple. It's very effective."

"It's mango and jacaranda," Sasha corrected her, and went to a chest of drawers for a hair dryer. "I painted it myself."

"I'm genuinely impressed. Do you hope to be an interior decorator when you grow up?"

Sasha handed over the hair dryer. "No, a doctor," she said, and walked out of the room.

Megan stood there for a full ten seconds, open-mouthed.

"Mommy! I'm *cold!*" Celeste called.

Megan glanced around the room once more, then returned to the downstairs bathroom.

Wrapped in a huge towel, Celeste bounced on Megan's bed while Megan changed into her jeans, then dried what she could of her clothes by holding the dryer over her chest and moving it from side to side. It only took a few minutes, then she sat on the bed and turned the dryer on Celeste's long tresses.

As she combed out Celeste's nearly dry hair, a knock sounded at the door. "Come in!" she called, then looked up, expecting it to be Sasha coming to admonish her again, perhaps for leaving the bathroom a mess, or Daisy to have a chat.

She was startled to see Luke. Based on what he'd said

earlier, she'd assumed he'd never set foot in her room again.

"People are arriving," he said, "How long do you think you'll be?"

"I'm just finishing Celeste's hair and then I'll be right out."

"Mommy's makin' me pretty, Daddy," Celeste said. "Leave us girls 'lone, okay?" she added primly.

LUKE BLINKED. HE HADN'T realized how much his little girl was growing up. She'd taken charge of the situation, dismissing him in favor of doing "girl things" with her new mommy. Still…it was nice to see them together.

If only he and his son could share some "guy things…" Then maybe they could grow closer. A thought occurred to him, something that might help that wish come true.

"I'm leaving," he said, and bent to kiss Celeste's forehead. His face passed Megan's as he straightened. She didn't exactly pull back from his gaze, but she sure wasn't turning her face toward him for some of the same attention.

BY THE TIME CELESTE pronounced that Megan had finished with her hair and gotten dressed, the house was full of children and adults.

"Megan, there you are!" Beth greeted her as they entered the living room. She planted a welcoming kiss on her cheek.

Megan relaxed almost immediately. She'd been dreading the moment she had to meet the rest of Luke's brothers and their wives, but Beth had effectively broken the ice.

Beth took her hand and drew her into the group. "Everyone, this is Megan. Luke, maybe you should do the introductions."

Matt was holding Sarah. He kissed Megan and looked into her eyes, his expression one of concern. "I hope you're settling in?"

Megan nodded mutely. What had Matt's look meant? Had Luke told his brother they were already having problems? She pushed the thought away and turned to smile at the other occupants of the room.

"This is my brother, Jack," he said, indicating a tall, well built man with jet-black hair and brilliant blue eyes who came forward and shook her hand. Megan noticed that his hand was large and calloused, his grip firm. *Jack is a carpenter.* Luke's words rang in her head.

"Welcome to our family, Megan. I hope you and Cody will be happy here," he said, then stepped back.

"I'm happy to meet you, Jack," Megan said, glancing across at Cody, who stood scowling in the corner of the room. Apparently, he'd already met his new relatives and passed judgment on them. They were far too clean-cut and warmhearted for his liking, she guessed. "Have you met my son, Cody?" she asked, sending him a warning look. "Cody's learning to ride, thanks to Daisy's patience, aren't you?"

"Yeah," Cody said, lightly punching Daisy's shoulder. "Hey, kid. You wanna play catch?" he asked her.

Daisy gazed up at him; she obviously loved having someone around who didn't think doing your hair, playing with dolls or cooking and cleaning was the greatest thing on earth. "Yeah!" she said, and they disappeared outside.

Megan didn't realize she'd been holding her breath

until the screen door slammed behind them. At least Cody had made a firm friend in Daisy. They'd be good for each other. As long as Cody didn't swear around her.

Luke was saying, "And this is my brother, Will."

Another man, almost the same height and coloring as Matt, stepped forward and pulled her into a bear hug. Megan's breath left her in a *whoosh* and then a woman's voice said sternly, "Will O'Malley, leave that poor girl alone!"

He obeyed and moved back, grinning sheepishly to allow a woman with green eyes and an unruly tumble of dark auburn curls to come toward Megan. "Please forgive my husband, Megan. He has no idea how to behave in company."

Megan looked at Will, who could barely wipe the smile off his face, and thought, *He knows exactly how to behave to get his wife's attention.* "It's fine. I just haven't been hugged quite so…enthusiastically in a long time." Megan laughed, breaking the tension.

"I'm Becky, by the way," the other woman said, then gave Megan a hug that wasn't quite as ferocious as her husband's. "I'm so glad Luke found you and Cody and brought you home." She looked around the room. "Now our family's almost complete."

At Megan's frown of confusion, Becky explained. "We think Jack and Adam need to find themselves wives, but as Adam barely talks to anyone, he's not going to manage it on his own. If we could only get him to move closer to home…"

Megan grinned at Becky's desire to matchmake for a reluctant but much-loved brother-in-law. "I take it he's the strong, silent type?" she said, and noticed Luke shifting uncomfortably beside her.

Becky nodded. "Oh, boy! Is he ever. Just like Luke. *Worse* than Luke. Much worse than Luke. At least Luke can carry on a conversation. Sometimes." She dug Luke in the ribs.

Becky was right; Luke *was* the strong, silent type. He rarely wasted words. Rarely smiled, too, as though watching and waiting, gauging what was going on before committing himself. He hadn't been like that when she'd known him before. He was far more gregarious back then.

"And these are your children, Nick and Lily?" Megan asked Becky, gesturing toward the other two occupants of the room—a boy with his mother's red hair and vivid blue eyes and a baby, sleeping in her carrier—hoping she'd got their names correct. Becky beamed, clearly pleased that Megan had remembered her children's names.

"Nicolas, this is your aunt Megan," Becky said to the boy who was kidding around with Sasha.

It was probably the first time Megan had seen the girl smile. Obviously, she liked her cousin.

"Hi, Aunt Megan," he said, approaching her and shaking her hand.

Megan noted that he walked with a slight limp and wondered about it. "Hello, Nick," she said. "I'm pleased to meet you."

Cody and Daisy had rushed in the back door moments earlier, and she introduced Cody to everyone who hadn't met him yet, cringing at his sullen attitude but reluctant to call him on it in front of his new relatives.

Megan looked to her husband for guidance when the

room fell silent. When Luke didn't respond, she cleared her throat and glanced back at the gathering. "Well, I suppose I should ask, 'Won't you all sit down?' so please—" she held her arms out, taking in the well-worn furniture of the living room. "Make yourselves comfortable. I think Sasha and Celeste have prepared some treats for you." She glanced at Sasha, who prodded Celeste and disappeared into the kitchen along with Nick.

Megan sat in a large, comfortable chair, and after Luke had finished serving drinks to everyone, he perched on the arm of it.

The children returned from the kitchen and passed some appetizers around. Sarah was standing unsteadily by her father, clinging to Matt's leg.

Becky reached into the duffel bag she'd brought with her. "I brought over some clothes of mine that don't fit me anymore. Beth said your own belongings won't get here for a few days. Although looking at you, I'm sure all my clothes will be too baggy. I don't think I've been as slim as you since I was about twelve." She laughed and said, "If ever!"

Megan observed Becky's generous curves and envied her. She knew Becky's comments were meant in jest, but they stung a little all the same. "Thank you, but I don't think I'll need them. My stuff should get here soon. Until then I can manage with what I have."

Beth dug into her bag, too, and produced a small pile of neatly folded clothes, saying, "But wait, as they say in the ads, there's more." She gave the pile to Megan with a smile. "I hope you can find something to fit you here, too, Megan."

Megan nodded and accepted the clothes, feeling like

someone's poor relative. "I...I really don't think I'll need them," she said again.

"'Course you will," Sasha piped up. "You don't even have a *nightgown*. Daddy had to put you to bed in your underwear last night."

Megan gasped. She'd never felt so totally mortified in her life. Her face was so hot it must be glowing beet red and her lips trembled at the accusatory tone of Sasha's voice. Why was Sasha doing this to her—and in front of everybody?

"E-excuse me," she finally managed to say, and got awkwardly to her feet. "I'll just put these in my room." She turned and fled down the hallway.

She threw the clothes on her bed. "Charity case!" she muttered angrily. "Little brat! And the rest of them think I'm a charity case!"

"Megan?"

Megan turned at the sound of Beth's voice. She'd walked into Megan's room and had obviously heard every word she'd said. Her face held pity.

Megan brushed at an errant tear. "Don't look at me like that!" she said. "I don't need to be treated like this!"

Beth closed the door, then urged Megan over to the bed and sat down beside her. "I'm sorry, that was all my fault. Becky and I didn't mean any harm by it. Matt told me you didn't have anything other than the clothes you wore to court and a pair of jeans and a shirt you bought on the way out of New York. He said the moving company could be a week, so I'm afraid I mentioned it to Becky this morning." She placed her hand on Megan's arm. "It's all my fault," she said again. "Please don't blame Becky. We meant it in the kindest way. We're sisters now," she said gently.

Megan reached over to grab a tissue to dab at her tears, angry at herself for letting her emotions surface like this. "I didn't need Sasha pointing out how incompetent I was. I guess that's what set me off," she murmured.

Beth placed her arm around Megan's shoulders. "I'm afraid Sasha's mother wasn't the kindest person on earth and Sash has inherited her sharp tongue. I apologize for her behavior, but you'll see—she'll come around. This is going to be a big adjustment for her, having another woman in the house full-time. She's really a very generous child underneath all her bluster."

Megan nodded. "I know. But she likes to stab me every now and then with her cattle prod."

Beth laughed. "That's better! Keep a sense of humor and you'll be fine. As for Becky, she was just treating you like one of us." She squeezed Megan's shoulder. "We're all so overjoyed to have you in our family and for Luke to have found his son. We'd never want you to feel uncomfortable about being here."

Nodding, Megan blew her nose. There was a knock at the door and then Sasha called, "Can I come in?"

Megan looked dubiously at Beth, who squeezed her shoulder again. "Give her time," she whispered.

Megan stiffened her shoulders and got up off the bed to open the door. Sasha stood there twisting her hands. Megan had never seen her nervous before.

"My daddy said I should apologize to you for what I said."

Megan let out a sigh. "If you want to apologize, that's

fine, Sasha, but don't feel you should just because your father told you to."

Sasha seemed confused by that remark, glanced at Beth, and then back at Megan. "Yeah, well, I'm sorry. Okay?" she said with a touch of belligerence.

"I'm sorry, too, Sasha, for making a mess of the clothes you'd taken so much time over. I should have changed into my jeans to bathe Celeste. I'd forgotten how much water a four-year-old can kick out of a tub."

Sasha nodded solemnly. "Well, are you going to come outside with everyone now?" she asked.

Megan turned to Beth, who smiled encouragingly. She turned back to Sasha. "Lead the way," she said.

EVERYONE HAD MOVED outside to the back lawn. The sun was setting in magnificent colors behind the mountains and the older children had a makeshift game of baseball going on. The adults either sat or stood around talking. When Luke noticed Megan standing on the bottom step of the porch, he came toward her and caught both her hands in his. "Are you okay?" he asked, his voice full of concern.

"I'm fine. A minor misunderstanding, that's all. I hope I didn't spoil the party by being so stupid."

Luke squeezed her hands gently between his. "I'm truly sorry about what Sash said. And my sisters-in-law just wanted you to feel welcome."

"I realize that now and I'll try not to be so sensitive in the future...."

Luke cupped her cheek and touched her lips with his. When she pulled back, startled, he said under his breath, "Work with me here, will you?" he said gruffly. "I don't need my wife treating me as though I'm repugnant to her."

Taken aback by his admission that he needed them to maintain an outward show of togetherness—and needing to feel Luke's touch—she looped her arms around his neck and pressed her lips to his.

She wasn't prepared for the explosion of sensation and feeling that shot through her body as their mouths met again and Luke pulled her closer. Standing as she was on the bottom step, Megan wasn't that much shorter than Luke. Through the thickness of his jeans and hers, she could feel the hard evidence of his desire. It both shocked and surprised her. She'd thought Luke was indifferent to her after his declaration earlier and his plea to pretend to the rest of the family that they were happily married. She hadn't thought he could desire her.

She leaned close and Luke placed his arms around her, deepening the kiss. Megan closed her eyes and let the sensations assail her, allowing her fingers to comb through his hair.

The catcalls and whistles from the garden permeated the erotic haze surrounding her and when Luke ended the kiss, she was breathless and wishing they were alone. He might not love her, but God help her, she loved him, had never stopped loving him. She'd take every morsel of affection she could grasp.

"Talk about a cold shower," Luke muttered and took several deep breaths as if trying to control his reaction to her. "Maybe we'd better join the others?"

Megan nodded, hoping her blush of embarrassment wasn't visible in the evening light and let him lead her to where the others waited.

"We don't need to light the barbecue, we'll just sizzle

the steaks on you two," Will declared, and laughed up-roariously. The others joined in and soon Megan's self-consciousness was forgotten.

THE EVENING WENT WELL. The food was consumed with gusto, the children played happily together, and by the end of the night, Cody had come out of his shell and was talking to the other kids, especially Becky's son, Nicolas. Celeste had spent almost the entire evening sitting on Megan's lap, telling everyone that her new mommy had done her hair. The child's acceptance of her had eased the way for Megan and she was grateful for it.

The only sour note came when the dessert had been served and Becky had made a remark about giving Megan the recipe for ambrosia, saying, "Luke won't be able to keep his hands off you when you feed him that!"

Sasha, sitting with the children, had overheard it and announced, "That won't be a problem, since they don't even share the same room."

Megan had gasped with horror and looked around the gathering. There was pity on the faces of Beth and Matt, who knew they didn't share a room, but Will, Jack and Becky hadn't been aware of the fact until now and all eyes seemed to be boring into her, curious to know what was going on.

"Sasha, go to your room," Luke said quietly.

"But, Dad, it's true!" she protested.

"Go to your room."

She stood and threw her napkin on the table. "It's true! They don't sleep together!" she told the gathering. "I don't even believe they're married!"

"Go to your room, Sasha!" Luke's voice rose dangerously.

Megan put a restraining hand on his arm. "Luke, please. Don't make a scene. Leave her be," she pleaded softly. Megan hadn't missed the shocked look on Cody's face at Sasha's outburst, she was embarrassing him so much.

"Gosh!" Becky said, and laughed heartily. "Is that what you're worrying about, Sash? You think your daddy and Megan aren't properly married, so it isn't right for them to share a room?" She glanced around the rest of the adults at the table, as if trying to garner their agreement.

Megan was grateful that Becky was attempting to turn Sasha's reaction around to seem less offensive and downright rude. Even Cody seemed to have relaxed.

"Well, we'll just have to have another wedding," Becky declared. "A *real* one this time, with pretty bridesmaids and a ceremony and a big party afterward!"

That effectively diffused the situation and got the children involved, with each of them yelling excitedly about what they wanted to contribute and who was going to be wearing what. All except Sasha. Megan was staggered by their enthusiasm. Becky sure knew how to stir up a crowd.

"I can ask Mom and Pop to get back here by next weekend," Matt offered.

"And naturally I'll perform the honors, seeing as I'm a qualified judge," Becky said.

"I'll call everyone Luke's ever known and invite them." That was Jack. He turned to Megan, smiling. "And I'll make the calls for you, too."

Megan shook her head. Her family wouldn't be

interested in coming and she had very few friends in New York, certainly none who could afford to travel all the way to Colorado. She felt Luke's hand reach for hers beneath the table and that small action heartened her. She stiffened her back and spoke up. "I appreciate that, Jack, but Cody and I are part of your family now, so I hope your friends will be ours."

When Luke brought her hand to his lips, Megan knew she'd said the right thing without having to reveal to his family the painful circumstances of her estrangement from her own.

"I can't help out much," Luke said. "I'll be up at the Cattlemen's Convention and sale in Wyoming until Saturday morning."

"Never fear!" Beth assured him. "The O'Malley women are here. When you get back on Saturday, all you'll have to do is scrub up, put on your tux and get out onto the back lawn in time for the ceremony."

Luke grinned. "Sounds good to me." He looked at Megan. "Is all this okay with you? They're not railroading you into anything you don't want, are they?"

Megan had lost her voice since Luke had lifted her hand to his lips. She shook her head, mutely. He was leaving her by herself on the ranch next week? And she was only finding out about it *now?*

Matt slapped his hands on the table. "I'm going to go call Mom and Pop while the kids clean up the table and load the dishwasher."

"Aw, Uncle Matt!" they cried in unison.

Matt held up his hands to stay their protests. "Come on, guys, your moms have worked hard to prepare this feast and your fathers have worked hard eating it, so it's your turn. I'll give a ride in my patrol car to the kid who works the hardest."

That had children flying all over, clearing tables, scraping plates, carrying things to the kitchen.

Becky watched them all disappear into the house, Matt bringing up the rear to go and phone his parents. "What a guy." She sighed. "Sometimes I wish I'd married that man."

Will guffawed and grabbed his wife around the waist. "If you'd married him, then I wouldn't have a terrific sister-in-law like Beth."

Becky considered that for a moment, then nodded sagely. "You're right. Good thing I was prepared to put up with second best." Then she squealed when Will threw her up over his shoulder, fireman-style, and carried her into the house, Becky laughing and pummeling his back all the way.

Jack and Beth collected the remaining glasses and hurried after them, laughing as Will tickled Becky, making her squeal more.

Megan watched them go, longing for the happiness and love the other couples shared. She'd been alone for so many years, depending only on herself, she found it comforting to acknowledge that such closeness between families could exist. But now, having spent the evening with the O'Malleys, she wanted that camaraderie for herself.

"What are you thinking?" Luke asked beside her.

Megan turned to him, startled by the intense tone of his voice. Darkness had descended as they'd eaten dinner and now the garden was lit only by bamboo torches, placed at strategic points around the perimeter, and candles on the table. Luke leaned forward, cupping his hand around the nearest candle and blew it out, then moved closer to Megan.

Instinctively, she pulled back. She wasn't ready for this, despite what had happened earlier. Despite wanting to deepen their relationship. Her reaction had been unthinking—self-protective.

Luke gave a hiss of disgust, got up from the table and strode into the house.

Chapter Eight

Megan tossed and turned most of the night. She'd handled things badly and upset Luke when she hadn't meant to. She'd seen the passion flare in his eyes. Did Luke have genuine feelings for her? Megan was afraid to ask. Afraid of the answer—either way!

When she stumbled tiredly into the kitchen the next morning, it was deserted. The house was silent. Apparently, everyone had already eaten breakfast and gone. A note from Luke was propped against the vase of flowers in the middle of the table. Megan opened it and read.

> We've gone to help at Matt and Beth's house. Cody, too. Ben will give you directions. Keys are in the car.

Megan stared at the note. He must still have been angry when he wrote it, she thought. No greeting, no signature, just a curtly written note as if he didn't care whether she showed up or not. Well, she wouldn't, because she didn't have a driver's license. In fact, she hadn't driven since she'd dropped out of college. That was a legacy of living in New York—no need for a car and nowhere to park one, anyway.

She had toast and a cup of coffee for breakfast, then went in search of anything she could do around the house to fill in the time until everyone returned. The house was neat; the only thing that might need cleaning were the worn covers on the sofas. "Uh-uh!" she said. "Forget it. Little Miss Sourpuss's going to complain, no matter what I do."

Megan headed back into the laundry, seeking clothes to wash or iron. Everything was spotlessly clean, pressed clothes hanging, waiting to be taken to various rooms. Megan could work out by the sizes who owned what, so she took them to their respective rooms and hung them up. That done, she found some carrots and brought them to the stable, making friends with the various horses. Ben, the ranch hand, wasn't anywhere in sight.

"So much for getting directions from Ben," she muttered, and stroked Sage's nose. The horse nickered, pressing her muzzle to Megan's face. "What do you think of that husband of mine, Sage? I can't figure him out, that's for sure." The mare nodded as if agreeing.

The sound of a truck pulling up outside and a honking horn had Megan racing to the barn door, hoping it was Luke returning to say he'd forgiven her and that he wanted them to try and be friends...and maybe lovers.

Her face fell when she didn't recognize the vehicle. The door opened and Beth climbed down. "Hey, Megan!" she called toward the house.

"Over here." Megan waved.

Beth turned in her direction. "Is everything all right? Luke sent me over to get you. He got worried when you didn't turn up. You don't look too happy," Beth observed as Megan neared the truck.

Megan shrugged her shoulders. "I didn't know we

were supposed to be visiting you today. Otherwise, I would've made sure Luke included me rather than let me sleep in."

Beth laughed. "I doubt you'd call it *visiting*. Our house isn't built yet. All the boys come over on weekends and work on it. We don't have a phone, and cell coverage isn't great over there, or one of us would've called you." She grinned. "You should see the guys. They're all so busy trying to show us women how macho they are. Anyway, when I asked Luke where you were, he suggested I come by. Hop in and I'll drive you."

Megan climbed into the truck, then got down again.

"Where are you going?" Beth called as she ran to the front door.

"To lock up." She stopped and bit her lip. She didn't even have a key to the house. Some wife!

"Don't worry about it," Beth said. "Luke never locks up."

Megan climbed back in. "I guess there are a lot of things I need to learn about living in the country," she said.

Beth reversed the truck and headed toward the gates. "You'll learn quickly enough. I came from L.A.—lived there all my life. I've been here less than two years and yet I feel so much a part of the place that L.A. seems like a distant memory."

"Did you meet Matt in L.A.?" Megan asked.

Beth turned out of the gate and gunned the truck down the gravel road. "No. I was pregnant with Sarah when I moved here. I met Matt the night I had her."

"You're kidding!" Megan faced her. "You mean to

tell me he isn't Sarah's natural father? That's hard to believe."

Beth concentrated on the road as she took a left turn and entered another valley. "I know. But I was actually widowed. I crashed my car into a snowbank on the way to the hospital. Matt rescued me, drove like a maniac to the hospital and stayed with me while Sarah was born."

"That's so romantic!"

Beth smiled at her. "Matt doesn't remember it quite that way!"

For the rest of the trip Beth told Megan about how she and Matt had ended up getting married. Megan was enchanted with her story. She could tell from the first moment how much Matt adored his beautiful wife and their daughter. *Oh, to have a love like that,* Megan thought, not for the first time.

"Give him a chance, will you?"

"What do you mean?"

Beth looked across at her, eyes full of compassion. "I know it's not going so well between you two. In spite of that hot kiss on the back porch last night."

Megan slumped in her seat. "Does *everyone* know that was just for show?"

Beth patted her thigh. "Relax. In spite of Sasha's little routine, everybody—except Matt and me—assumes that things are fine between you."

"In that case, the others will start picking up clues pretty soon, too." Why had she thought they could make this marriage work?

For Cody, she reminded herself.

Beth turned in at another gate, and as they made their way along the drive, Megan could see the frame of a substantial log home coming into view. Children were running through the fields chasing one another while the men worked. Becky was setting up lunch on long tables in the sun. "Oh, it's lovely," she breathed. "What a magnificent setting...and home!"

Beth pulled up beside the other vehicles. "Thank you. Will owned this ranch land. He carved it into ten-acre ranchettes and sold it off to save some old buildings in town. I'll have to take you down there to see what they've done. I'm sure you'll find it interesting. Will and Jack have really performed a miracle restoring the old buildings." She got out of the truck. "Matt decided to invest in one of the lots here."

Megan nodded approvingly. "Then he has exceptional taste in land—as well as wives." She smiled across at Beth. "I can imagine how it'll look, with lots of glass on this side to take in the views." She nudged Beth excitedly. "Walk me through it, okay? Tell me where everything's going to go. But who designed it?"

"Matt...with a bit of help from me. I'm an architect."

Megan realized she knew so little about her in-laws. If nothing else, she intended to make it her mission over the next couple of days to learn as much as she could. Maybe then she'd feel more like part of the family.

"Hey, there!"

Megan turned to see Luke approaching with his arms outstretched. He threw them around her and pulled her into a hug.

"I've missed you," he said, placing his hands on either side of her face and kissing her thoroughly.

Beth's words swirled in Megan's head. She and Matt knew it was just a performance. Well, she was going to make damn sure no one else did. Wanting to make up for rejecting his advances the previous night, she returned his kiss, her hands sliding up Luke's muscled back to hold him close. Only his T-shirt separated them and she wished it wasn't there. Wished her hands were gliding over his bare skin...

"Mom, stop it," Cody hissed from behind her, and Megan broke off the embrace.

"Cut it out," he muttered angrily. "You're embarrassing me!"

Feeling slightly unsteady on her feet, Megan held on to Luke as they both turned to face their son. Luke's hand rested possessively on her waist and Megan was pleased to note that he was as breathless as she was.

Luke found his voice first. "Cody. Your mom and I are newlyweds. No one else is embarrassed about this. Look around you." He raised his arm to encompass everyone who'd politely returned to their business.

"They were all staring before and I don't like it."

"Then get over it," Luke said harshly. His arm still around Megan, he led her toward the house.

Megan was surprised by Luke's tone. She halted and placed her hand on his chest. "It's not necessary to speak to him like that. He has a right to express his opinion."

Luke glared down at her. "He only talks to me when he wants to criticize or tell me not to do something that might offend him. I've had a gutful of it. It's about time he learned not to be such a spoiled mama's boy."

Megan's couldn't believe she'd just heard that. "*Spoiled mama's boy?* How *dare* you!" she said, and turned away so the others wouldn't see her stormy expression.

Luke caught her elbow and started walking with her down the driveway, away from everyone else. "Look," he said, and she could hear the exasperation in his voice. "I've had nothing but grief from that kid since he got here. He'll talk to my brothers, but whenever *I* try to talk to him, he clams up."

"Then maybe you'd be better off if I took my *mama's boy* and we got out of your li—"

Luke spun her around to face him. "Don't you even *think* about it," he said through clenched teeth. "You try to deny me access to my son like you have for the past fourteen years and I'll pursue you through the courts and get sole custody of him."

Fear tightened Megan's chest. "No!" she managed to gasp as tears spilled from her eyes. What hope would she have against Luke and his money? He could hire the best attorneys, who would immediately point to the fact that she was such a bad mother their son had almost ended up in juvenile detention.

Luke released her arm and ran a hand through his hair. "I'm sorry. I didn't mean that. I was letting off steam. Cody seems to be going out of his way to make my life hell and then rubbing it in by being nice to my brothers."

"And with your caveman tactics, who can blame him?"

"Megan, I'm trying here, okay? I *want* to be his dad, but it's damned hard when he keeps pushing me away."

"Just like Sasha keeps pushing *me* away," Megan said. She saw the deep frown lines across his forehead and ached to reach up and smooth them away. She believed

Luke genuinely wanted to be a dad to Cody, but he was going about it all wrong.

Aware that they had an audience now that everyone was gathering around the tables for lunch, she stepped back, gesturing in her son's direction. "Don't try so hard, then. Let him come to you. You don't have to put up with him criticizing you, but don't bite back. Turn it around and maybe ask him how *he* feels something should be done." She smiled. "That'll shock him, because the truth is, he's in an environment that's so foreign to him, he's rebelling against it, by taking it out on you."

Luke caught her hand and brought it to his mouth, placing a gentle kiss on her palm. As warmth spread through her, she couldn't help thinking, *If only he meant that kiss, instead of playacting for the benefit of his family.*

"Okay," he said hoarsely, as though the kiss had affected him as much as her. "Just promise never to threaten me with leaving."

Megan studied him for a moment. She'd never seen Luke so vulnerable, never considered it possible that he'd fear her walking out.

She squeezed his hand in reassurance. "Don't call him a mama's boy, okay?"

Luke nodded. "I know. That was unfair." She could see in his eyes the love he had for their son. "It can't have been easy for you, being both mother and father to him, and it can't have been easy for him, either, and I'm sorry about that. But I think you've tended to indulge him rather than take a firmer stand."

She felt her anger flare, but before she could vent her feelings over that comment, Luke took her in his arms so it looked as though they were sharing lovers words rather than angry ones. "Let's not get into this now," he said, "but we need to talk when we get home, okay?"

Realizing that arguing would get them nowhere—other than into a potential full-scale argument in front of a dozen curious onlookers—Megan nodded and smiled, the kind of smile a woman would give her husband if they'd shared a secret. Luke smiled back and kissed her on the lips, then turned to walk her back to the rest of the group.

The children collected their lunches and went to sit on blankets spread beneath the trees on the other side of the house. The adults sat at the table Becky had set.

"Where were you, Megan?" Will asked. "Luke thought you must still be sleeping and sent Beth to get you."

Megan flushed. "I…I don't have a driver's license. In fact, I haven't driven a car for nearly fifteen years. I'm not sure I'd remember how."

Jack laughed heartily. "You'll remember! Or put it this way, you'd *better* remember. Those little princesses need transport to dancing lessons, swimming lessons—"

"Don't forget Daisy's tae kwon do," Becky threw in.

"And all those birthday parties and sleepovers they get invited to," Matt said, rolling his eyes. "You'll feel like you're running a taxi service," he warned.

Megan fretted. What if it took her ages to be good enough to take her driving test? "I didn't need a car in New York," she explained, "so I let my license lapse."

"I'll give you a lesson after lunch if you'd like," Beth offered. "The roads around here are deserted. You'll be fine."

The rest of the lunch passed pleasantly, and when the men went back to work, Beth walked Megan through the house, pointing out the various rooms and discussing decor.

They returned to the living room, where Jack and Luke were creating a rock fireplace. "It's absolutely enchanting," she said. "I can't wait to see it when it's finished."

"Neither can I!" Beth said with a laugh. "We're living in a tiny cabin up on Blue Spruce Drive, and although it was cozy at first, now that we're accumulating furniture for this house, it's getting a little *too* cozy!"

Matt appeared out of nowhere and grabbed Beth in a bear hug, complete with bearlike noises. "What's the matter, wife? Complaining about my need to nest?"

Beth turned, slipping her arms around his neck, and Megan moved away to give them privacy. As she did, she was confronted by the sight of Luke, who'd removed his T-shirt. His back muscles, sheened with sweat, rippled as he lifted the slabs of stone and his biceps bulged with the effort.

He didn't seem to be aware of her but Megan couldn't stop staring….

This wasn't good. She could no more control her body's reaction to Luke than change the tides.

Beth saved her from drooling by suggesting they take that driving lesson now.

BETH WAS A PATIENT teacher, and by the time they drove back to the house two hours later, Megan felt her confidence returning.

"You should apply to take your test this week," Beth said as she climbed out of the vehicle. "I'll get the sheriff to set it up with the DMV if you like." She winked at Megan and they went to join the others. "If you'll excuse me, I think my little darling is hungry," Beth said as Matt met them, Sarah fussing in his arms.

After arranging with Matt to do her test later in the week, she went in search of Cody. He was behind the house digging a trench, working alongside his father. As if sensing her presence, Luke looked up and smiled.

"How'd it go?" he asked, jumping out of the trench.

"Matt's going to arrange for me to take my driving test. Beth says I'm ready and all I need to do is study the rules of the road. If all goes well, I should be driving the girls around in no time."

"That's great," he said, drawing her away. "Because we haven't had a chance to talk about the Cattlemen's Convention in Wyoming yet. I'll be leaving in the morning."

Megan folded her arms. "Leaving me stuck in the middle of nowhere with no way of getting around? What if something happens to the children?"

"Relax. One of the hands will be here to take care of you. He and Cody are switching places."

"What do you mean?"

"Cody's coming to Wyoming with me. He's looking forward to it."

Megan could feel her throat closing up with fear. "But he's never been anywhere without me before!"

Luke nodded. "In that case, isn't it time he did?"

"I...I need to think about this."

"What's to think about? We'll be back Saturday. It'll be a terrific opportunity for my son and me to get to know each other without you around."

"Excuse me?"

"Ah, let me rephrase that—"

"Don't bother!" Megan stormed over to where Cody was in the ditch. "Cody, you won't be going to Wyoming. I'll be enrolling you in school first thing in the morning."

"But I wanna go, Mom. School's dumb."

"School is *not* dumb, young man! You need to get your grades back up. You're going to school in the morning, whether you like it or not."

Megan was so enraged that Luke had taken over without talking to her first, she was trembling. And as for telling Cody he didn't have to go to school! Wasn't this one of the reasons for moving to Colorado? To make sure he *did* attend school? She felt Luke's hand on her shoulder and shrugged it off.

"Megan, if you'd let me finish... I was going to give you the good news that Cody's agreed to go to summer school to get his grades up. There's only a week of school left here in Colorado before summer vacation. He won't achieve anything much in a week, but he'd gain a wealth of experience from coming to the Cattlemen's Convention with me."

Megan's shoulders slumped. Luke was right, but she wasn't happy with the way he'd gone about it without consulting her first. At least no one else had witnessed the humiliating exchange between them. The rest of the O'Malleys had made themselves scarce.

She turned to face him. "If you're sure it will be of more benefit to him than school *and* that he'll really go to summer school, then I guess I can't object. But I don't like the sound of this arrangement of yours about the hand 'taking care of' the girls and me."

"Don't worry. Ben's been with our family for longer than I've been alive. He'll keep an eye on the ranch and your safety. Mrs. Robertson, our housekeeper, will be in every morning. She'll take the girls to school and pick them up, do any shopping, cook the evening meal and clean."

Megan felt completely redundant and couldn't help her sarcastic retort. "And what am I supposed to do while Mrs. Robertson has all the fun? Play the lady of the manor?

Luke looked shocked for a moment, then threw back his head and laughed. He hugged her to him and murmured, "You know, I think we're gonna be all right."

Megan enjoyed being held in his arms.

"It'll help Cody and me bond, and I thought you could use the time to find out how to continue your studies. I'll support you fully, whatever you decide."

Once again, Megan felt the protective cloak of Luke surrounding her, shielding her from all the concerns she'd had to face alone just a few days ago. She placed a hand on his arm and said, "You make sure you bring my son back to me in one piece, okay?"

"No, I'll bring *our* son back in one piece. And furthermore—" he dropped a kiss on the end of her nose "—I plan to bring him back as a man."

Chapter Nine

Luke and Cody spent the evening packing for their trip. Megan hadn't seen her son so animated in a very long time, probably not since she'd taken him to Six Flags Great Adventure in New Jersey years ago. They'd gone by bus and stayed at a nearby B and B. The weekend trip had cost her a week's pay and put her behind with the rent, but had been worth every penny.

"You'll call to let me know you're there safely, won't you?" she implored.

"Yes, Mom."

"And you'll call me every night, too?"

"Yes, Mom." Cody's voice held a touch of irritation as he continued packing.

"And you'll call if you don't feel safe?"

"Mom!" Cody looked up and sighed. As if sensing her fear, he came and placed his hands on her shoulders. The relief she felt at their warmth allowed her to release her pent-up breath. "You gotta let go, okay? I'll be fine. You know Luke won't let me out of his sight."

Megan was still trying to think of excuses to get Cody to change his mind about going. "I know this is a big adventure for you, honey. But I'm scared. We've never been apart this long before."

Luke chose that moment to enter Cody's room and ask, "All set, son?"

"I will be, once Mom leaves me alone to finish my packing." He gave her a pointed look.

Megan turned to make one last appeal to Luke, but he held up his hands. "Don't even think about trying to talk me out of this, Megan. Cody is coming with me. He *wants* to come with me. I could list about a hundred reasons this'll be good for him."

"Then I'll get a pen and paper and start *my* list of a hundred reasons it *won't* be," Megan said, about to leave the room, but Luke stopped her at the door. His grin made her anger rise. "This isn't funny," she protested. "I'm really upset about it."

Luke steered her out of the room and down the hallway. He opened a door at the end and gestured Megan through it.

As soon as she realized it was Luke's bedroom, she turned on her heel, intending to leave. Instead, she came up against his hard chest. He nudged the door closed with his foot and led her to the bed, where he sat her down.

Megan looked everywhere but at Luke. The room was furnished Western-style in masculine colors, lots of wood, leather, a hand-stitched quilt on the...bed. The enormous bed. The bed he'd no doubt shared with Tory.

She leaped off it and went to sit in the leather armchair by the window. Luke came over, knelt down in front of her and took her hands as she fidgeted with them in her lap.

"I wasn't laughing at *you*," he said. "I was smiling. In spite of your fussing over Cody, I know you're doing it because you love him. I only wish Tory had fussed over the girls even a fraction as much."

Megan's shoulders relaxed. "I'm worried," she admitted. "We've never been apart."

She swallowed painfully. "Except...except for the two times he ran away and spent the night out on the street. I guess that's really why I'm so scared."

"I know. I know." He paused. "Look at me," he said, obviously noticing she'd glanced out the window, afraid to hear what he had to say.

When she focused back on him, he told her, "I promise I won't let Cody come to any harm. I'll keep him with me at all times. I'll make sure he calls you every night, okay?"

Megan nodded slowly and he added, "But don't wait by the phone, because he won't have a moment to himself—other than maybe thirty minutes to call you at night."

"O...kay," she agreed.

"Honey." He leaned closer. "I'm not feeling any qualms about leaving you in charge of my three precious daughters. And the reason for that is, I trust you. You're a good mom."

Megan stared at him uncomprehending.

"That was a compliment."

Pleasure bloomed inside her. "I...I've never thought of myself that way. I...feel like I've been such a bad mother. A fail—"

He cut her off by touching his finger to her lips. "I've never believed that, and neither should you."

"My son nearly ended up in juvenile detention!" she said, leaping to her feet, needing to put space between them. Luke's bedroom felt far too intimate for her.

"But he didn't. And he never will. I know I said you were too indulgent, but I understand why. I—"

Luke was right. Angry with herself, but perversely needing to take it out on Luke, she said, "And don't you just love it that you rode in on your white charger and fixed everything?" she demanded. "Rescued the stupid heroine, too helpless to do anything for herself."

"Stop that!" He captured her flailing hands in his and held them firm. "I'm no fairy tale knight. And you're certainly not helpless! Where is this coming from?" he asked. "Why are you trying to make me feel like the bad guy here?"

Yes, why was she dumping on Luke? So she'd feel better about herself?

In her heart, she knew it was unfair to take it out on him, but he was such an easy target. "Because everything you do makes me feel like a failure," she confessed, hating the catch in her voice.

"Oh, honey!" He pulled her to him, wrapping his arms around her. "You're not a failure. I've never thought that, and I'm positive no one else has, either."

She shook her head, unable to find comfort in his embrace. "The look you gave me in Judge Benson's office said it all. You *loathed* me!"

LUKE DIDN'T REMEMBER thinking any such thing, but she seemed beyond convincing. All he could do was hold her and silently try to impart his strength, his respect for her and his gratitude for all she'd done for their son. The judge was right; beneath the bravado, Cody was a good kid. Lousy moms didn't raise good kids.

"I hate leaving while you're feeling like this," he murmured into her hair, enjoying the fresh-washed smell of it, the softness of her body against his. He drew back, knowing that in a moment he'd be reacting to her nearness. She was as skittish as a filly. Bringing her into his bedroom probably wasn't the best idea he'd had all day, but they needed privacy. Four active kids running around, a ranch to run and the fact that they weren't sharing a bed left them no time to talk in private. And now, while Megan was obviously feeling so insecure and he was heading to another state for most of the week, *definitely* wasn't the right time for taking their relationship to another level, emotionally more than physically. One that would convince her that he wanted this to be a real marriage.

And that reminded him…. "Are you okay about us getting married all over again on Saturday? I can put a stop to it, if you think it's too silly, or putting you under pressure."

She managed a smile. "Really? I can just see you telling Celeste it's off. Major tantrum, including some floor work, gallons of tears, screaming and slamming of doors."

Luke laughed and said, "I think you're right. Plus Daisy, in spite of pretending she's not interested in such girly events, would probably horsewhip me."

"Sasha would be overjoyed, however."

She would, but Luke had no intention of being pushed around by a twelve-year-old. "In the eyes of the law, we're already married, so that's irrelevant. But I'm not prepared to hurt Celeste or the rest of my family, especially my parents. They're cutting short their Alaskan trip to be here."

Megan chewed on her lip.

"What's wrong?"

"Let me get that pencil and paper. I need to list how many things I'm unsure of. Number one being how your parents are going to feel about Cody."

Luke shrugged, unable to understand her concerns. "They'll love him on sight."

"Yeah…I'm sure they'll be impressed by their grandson's strange hairstyle, piercings and bad attitude." She shuddered. "I really want him to get rid of them and look…*normal* when he meets them."

"Let me see what I can do. What's your next problem?"

"You're trying to do the white knight thing again."

"Sorry, can't help it. I own horses. Gotta use them for something."

Megan smiled at that and Luke relaxed. He felt repeating the ceremony wasn't necessary. But what he felt didn't matter. It was too important to too many people not to go through with it. And although he'd exchanged the traditional wedding vows in front of friends and family before, it would be Megan's first time. Brides liked all that pomp and circumstance, didn't they? Which brought him to another thought, something he had to address before he left for Wyoming. "My family and friends know about the wedding and are coming, but in spite of what you told Jack, I really think we should let your folks know."

"They won't want to come."

"Of course they will. Granted, you've had your differences in the past, but this should be a time of healing for your family. How about if I call them up and invite them out here? Your friends, too—"

"No!" she said, slashing her hands through the air. "In fifteen years, my family hasn't once made contact with me. They knew where to find me. And none of my friends could afford to fly out here even if they wanted to come." She'd had friends once, girls who could afford to fly anywhere in the world first class, but they'd dropped off the radar soon after Cody's birth, if not before.

"Then I'll pay their fares."

She rounded on him, fire in her eyes. "Luke! Stop the white knight act. We're going through with this for the benefit of your family, nothing more! I don't *need* anyone else here."

Luke contemplated her words, particularly the ones about not needing anyone. He had the feeling that Megan had cut herself off from so many people, she truly believed she didn't need anyone in her life. Didn't need anyone's help. Or love.

"Okay, have it your way," he said. But he'd already decided to find Megan's parents and invite them to their only daughter's wedding. Because family was everything to him. *Family* was the way to happiness.

Chapter Ten

Megan cursed her alarm when it woke her at five the next morning. She'd barely slept, worrying that Luke would go against her wishes and contact her parents to invite them to their wedding.

Although confident he'd never find them, she was still worried. Luke knew they'd lived in Boston while she was at school, but she doubted he'd have time to search the Boston phone book, calling every Montgomery there.

She'd heard from a distant cousin, who kept in sporadic contact, that her parents had retired to Florida several years ago. Her father had turned over his law firm to her brother. He'd also sold the family home for an undisclosed but reportedly exorbitant sum.

Megan hauled herself out of bed and into the shower, needing it to wake her so she could see Cody and Luke off. Feeling guilty for having overslept the past couple of mornings, she was going to make up for it by having breakfast waiting on the table by the time they came downstairs.

Twenty minutes later she headed for the kitchen, but Luke had beaten her to it. He was bent over, peering into the fridge, giving her a nice view of his butt. She was almost tempted to whistle. Maybe she would if they were on intimate enough terms to joke about anything sexual; instead, she cleared her throat.

He turned around and offered one of his rare smiles, warming her insides more than she felt comfortable with.

"Hi. You didn't need to get up," he said, closing the door with his foot as he took out milk and eggs.

"You were going to have breakfast and sneak off without saying goodbye?" she said.

"I was hoping to bring you breakfast in bed, wake you slowly and make love to you while you ate it."

Megan could feel the color leaving her face. She resisted the urge to clasp the back of a chair for support.

"Are you okay?" he asked, setting the eggs on the table and coming toward her. He pulled out a chair and pressed her shoulders until she sat.

"I...I'm fine, but please don't say things like that. One of the children could have walked in."

"The girls won't be up until at least six. And Cody was snoring his head off when I passed his room. He won't get up until I wake him."

"Then we're alone?" she asked, rising shakily and going to pour herself coffee, noticing that Luke had already brewed a pot and drunk half a cup himself.

"Probably not long enough for me to make love to you before breakfast," he teased, clearly enjoying himself.

"Luke."

"But one day soon, I hope we can."

She swallowed, facing him, the coffee cup held in front of her. "About...about our wedding night..."

He placed strips of bacon on the griddle. "Where

would you like to go?" he asked, obviously mistaking her intent.

She frowned. *Go?* "I thought we'd be staying here… at the ranch."

"We should have a honeymoon. I hoped we could escape for a few nights. My folks will be here, so they can take care of the kids. It'll give them a chance to get to know Cody. Without either of us around."

If Luke's parents weren't planning to continue their Alaskan holiday, that meant they'd be moving back into their quarters. And *that* meant the only place she could sleep was with Luke. For a fleeting moment, she thought about sharing Cody's room, but immediately discounted it. How would that look to everyone? Some marriage! Perhaps it would be better if they went away. Got separate rooms. Figured out how they were going to make this marriage work—or *appear* to work.

"All right."

"Do I detect a lack of enthusiasm for my plans?" He flipped the bacon and cracked eggs into another pan.

"I…don't know much about honeymoons. Can I leave the arrangements up to you?"

"My pleasure."

"But only for a couple of days," she hastened to say. "I don't want to be away from the children for too long."

He considered her carefully. "Okay. If that's all you want. I'll find something local. Sunny-side up or over easy?"

She handed him a plate and said, "Sunny-side up. Cody likes his scrambled."

"Done," he said, lifting two eggs onto her plate and passing her a toasted bagel. He placed the drained bacon onto her plate, too. "I already know how Cody likes his eggs since I made his breakfast the past two mornings."

"While I slept in," she said, feeling a lump in her throat.

He piled his own plate high with bacon, four eggs and two toasted bagels. Topped up both their coffees and joined her at the table. "You needed the sleep," he told her. "Don't feel bad about it."

Megan had read about people in emergency situations who found enormous physical strength or managed to carry on for hours rescuing people, and then once the emergency was over, they collapsed, as if the situation had completely drained their reserves. Although she couldn't compare her recent life with Cody to an emergency, her nerves had been on high alert for months. She'd barely slept, listening to see if Cody was sneaking out, getting into trouble. Worrying about him. And then, when Luke had taken over sharing the responsibility for Cody, it was as though her body had said, "Now you can rest," and she had.

They ate in silence, each thinking of the days ahead. A *thump* sounded from upstairs and Luke rolled his eyes. "Princess number two is awake. As you've probably noticed, Daisy never does anything quietly."

"I had noticed that," Megan said with a smile. "What would she like for breakfast?" she asked, standing and taking their plates to the sink.

"She'd like waffles, maple syrup and ice cream."

Megan looked at him, aghast. What a thing to feed a child for breakfast on a school morning! No wonder Daisy was so loud and hyperactive.

Luke got up and laid one hand on her shoulder. "Relax," he said. "She might *want* that for breakfast, but what she'll get is fruit juice, scrambled eggs and granola or a bagel."

Megan got eggs from the fridge and turned to Luke. "I take it these were laid by your own hens?"

"Yup."

"Um, when am I supposed to collect them? I've never been around chickens. Their beady eyes scare me. Will they attack me if I try to take their eggs?"

Luke roared with laughter, then sobered when he could see she was genuinely afraid. "Don't worry about them. That's one of Celeste's duties in the morning, but if you want, she'll teach you." He put out bowls for the granola, plus milk and honey, and started toasting more bagels.

Megan enjoyed watching him and wondered just how many meals Luke had prepared for his daughters over the years. From now on, she'd take over that duty, leaving him with one less burden on his busy mornings. She scrambled the eggs and added grated cheese—Cody's favorite way of having them. Plus, it sneaked in some extra protein. She also sliced tomatoes in half and set them on the griddle.

"I'll go and wake the others," Luke said, leaving her alone in the kitchen.

Megan poured the scrambled egg mixture into a pan and opened the back door to let in the freshness of the early morning. It was a little chilly, but the dryness of the mountain air made it seem bracing rather than cold. She gazed out at the dawn breaking over the distant mountains, then remembered the eggs and raced back to the stove to stir them before they burned.

"Here you go, pumpkin," she heard Luke say from behind her.

He was walking into the kitchen, a sleepy-looking Celeste on his hip, his arms protectively around her. Her heart seemed to expand at the sight and in that moment she knew with absolute certainty that her son would be safe with Luke. Sadness and guilt gnawed at her as she realized Luke had never been able to experience their son at that same age.

Luke might have claimed she was a good mother— something she still wasn't convinced of—but she was certain that he was a good father. A great father. He'd protect his children with his life. He'd protect her son from harm. Correction, *their* son.

He was about to place Celeste gently in her chair, but then she saw Megan and cried, "Mommy!" She thrust out her arms toward Megan, who took her from Luke with pleasure. Celeste snuggled her face against Megan's throat and sighed with a pleasure that sounded as if that was where she wanted to be more than anywhere in the world.

The rest of the children soon entered the kitchen. Daisy and Cody returned her greetings, but Sasha chose to ignore her and instead yanked out her chair, sat down and pulled the granola box toward her.

Megan was tempted to repeat her greeting, but decided against it. Perhaps Sasha wasn't a morning person. She could relate to that, since she used to love sleeping in. But that was a luxury she'd given up a long time ago.

Luke was about to open his mouth but Megan stopped him, saying, "I'm sorry, I cooked the eggs too soon. I'll make another batch." She'd forgotten about the granola, since Cody wasn't partial to it.

"I'll eat 'em," Cody said, reaching for the pan and dumping the entire contents onto his plate.

"Yuck! What's that stuff in the eggs?" Sasha demanded.

"It's called cheese, Sash," Luke explained patiently, rolling his eyes at Megan.

Since Celeste didn't want to let go of her, Luke took over making the new batch of scrambled eggs while the girls ate their granola.

"Well, I don't like it," Sasha sulked. "Don't put any in mine."

"Too late," Luke said, then dumped a handful of cheese into the mixture a good five seconds after Sasha had voiced her protest.

Cody wasted no time devouring his eggs, tomatoes and bagels, and was looking around for more to eat. Luke poured him some extra juice and asked if he'd like coffee. Cody seemed surprised, as if no one had ever asked him that. Which they hadn't. Megan didn't think it was a suitable drink for a fourteen-year-old.

"Okay?" Luke asked, holding the coffee carafe poised over a mug.

Megan appreciated his asking. "Okay, but make it weak," she said.

"Cool!" Cody said, and watched his father pour the coffee, then add some hot water. He sipped it and his nose wrinkled.

"Sugar might help," Luke suggested, pushing the bowl toward him.

Cody dumped in two spoonfuls, stirred and drank. A look of bliss crossed his face. "So *this* is what everyone raves about."

LUKE SMILED TO HIMSELF and decided that if his son hadn't tried something as relatively harmless as coffee, he probably hadn't been experimenting with street drugs, either, in spite of his tough-guy image. The knowledge filled him with hope that their trip wouldn't consist of him trying to keep Cody out of every back alley they passed in Cheyenne, searching for drugs. He hadn't seen a cigarette between his lips even once, although many of the hands smoked around the ranch during their breaks.

He had no doubt that Cody had probably tried cigarettes in his recent past, but at least he wasn't addicted to them.

Luke served the scrambled eggs to Daisy and Sash, completely ignoring his older daughter's protests. Daisy pronounced them delicious, finished hers and reached for Sash's plate. Sash smacked her hand, then picked up her fork and dug in.

Luke couldn't hide his smile as he looked across the table at Megan. They were going to make it as a family; he was more determined about that than anything else in his life.

He drank his coffee and glanced around the table, taking in the scene, storing it for later, when he was feeling lonely during his trip. Except this time he'd have one of his kids along for company. He'd always imagined Daisy would be the first of his children to accompany him to the Cattlemen's Convention. He wondered how she was feeling about that, not being first.

He watched her, eyeing Sash's eggs as she forked them into her mouth. Nothing seemed to faze his second—make that *third*—child. Strange how he'd have to get used to the new family dynamic. The birth order.

He wondered how he would've felt if an older child had suddenly turned up in the midst of his own family. How would *he* have felt being relegated to second child when he'd been so used to being the oldest? He decided to allocate some special time to spend with Sash when he and Megan got back from their honeymoon. Perhaps Sash was jealous and that was part of the reason she was being so disagreeable. Maybe with Cody gone, she'd return to her usual sweet-natured self.

Then he saw Sash glaring at Megan and thought perhaps not.

Celeste, of course, had had no problem accepting not only a new mother, but also an older brother. In fact, his youngest child had been the glue that had held the family together over the past few stormy days. She loved and accepted Megan as her mother and, judging by the way Megan had slipped so easily into mothering Celeste, the feeling was mutual.

Cody had the look of the O'Malley men, but not quite the temperament. All the O'Malley brothers— apart from Will—had been conformists. Working at respected professions or trades, never giving their parents a moment's worry.

Although their mom maintained that Will was responsible for every gray hair on her head—of which there were few, since she was a blonde. It was their father who'd gone steel gray. Proof of Will's antics and itinerant lifestyle as a ski movie actor before he'd settled down to respectability with the town judge.

Luke wasn't sure Cody hadn't already added a few more gray hairs to his own head. These past few days he'd noticed that his temples seemed grayer. But that might also be a result of looking in the mirror more often—to make sure he appeared presentable enough for Megan.

The girls finished their breakfast and, amid noisy chatter and clattering dishes, cleared the table and started loading the dishwasher. "Leave that for me," Megan told them as she got up to help, Celeste still clinging to her neck.

Luke took a moment to drink in the sight of them together, then rose to take Celeste from her arms and put her in a chair at the table. His daughter whined but complied. He prepared her granola and sat with her while she ate. Slowly. He avoided glancing at his watch, knowing it upset Celeste when he counted down the minutes till he had to leave. But he and Cody needed to get on the road, and soon.

"Are you going to help Megan around the house this week, sweetie?" he asked, then cursed himself because Celeste dropped her spoon and began to answer him in long and breathless detail.

"We've got a few things planned," Megan said, as if she knew how to keep Celeste eating. "But you'll need to finish breakfast, Celeste, before we can start."

Luke glanced up at Megan, nodded and mouthed "thanks," then returned to watching Celeste eat. He kept up a one-sided monologue, careful not to ask any questions until she'd finished.

Luke was already missing his daughters. But if he was honest with himself, he was missing his wife, too.

He needed to get moving. Cody had come downstairs with his bag and loaded it into the truck. He was now out in the yard, reversing the Ford 350 up to the gooseneck trailer they'd be using to bring home a prize bull he'd arranged to buy from a friend in Wyoming. Orion, one of his old bulls, wasn't as virile as he used to be and needed to be replaced. Instead of using artificial insemination like many other ranchers, Luke preferred to breed the old-fashioned way.

He smiled at that, thinking about his upcoming honeymoon. He intended to make love to his wife—the old-fashioned way. Only this time he'd make sure he took plenty of condoms.

"What are you grinning about?" Megan asked, waking him from his musings.

"Trust me, wife," he said gruffly. "You don't want to know." He rose from his seat. "Time for us to hit the road. Will you see us off?"

"OF COURSE," MEGAN SAID, wiping her hands on a cloth and following him out the door, wondering exactly what Luke was smiling about and feeling a strangely uplifting sense of belonging when he'd called her *wife*. Her feminist sensibilities should have had her protesting his proprietorial remark, but instead, all she felt was pleasure. A sense of belonging in the nicest possible way.

The girls were outside watching Cody reverse the truck up to the trailer. Daisy yelled one set of instructions, while Sasha yelled the opposite. Cody was obviously learning how to handle his sisters, because he closed the window to block out their voices and expertly used the rear-vision mirrors to complete his mission.

Pleased that her son was already so accomplished at what she knew to be a difficult task, Megan turned to Luke with a smile and found him standing right behind her, his hands raised slightly as if he was about to put them around her. He lowered them and stepped back.

"I...I'm amazed at how quickly he's picked up driving," she remarked.

"He's a natural. I'm sure he'll get his license the first time he tries."

"You won't let him drive to Wyoming on the highway, will you?"

It was back again, that fear she couldn't completely suppress. The fear that something bad might happen to Cody because she wasn't there to watch over him. "I'm sorry, that was a stupid question and totally uncalled for."

"Apology accepted. And for what it's worth, I'll only be allowing him to drive on private property while we're away. I've promised him that once he turns fifteen he can do driver's ed at school."

Startled, Megan said, "I'll bet that won him over. They didn't offer it at his school."

He touched the end of her nose. "Add that to your list of good reasons for moving to Colorado."

"I don't have a list for that," she said.

"Make one," Luke murmured, then kissed her.

Megan had expected a farewell peck on the cheek, but Luke covered her lips and moved his mouth over hers as he slid his arms around her. She tentatively lifted her hands to his hips, hoping the girls wouldn't choose this moment to look back at the house and see them making out. For making out they were. Luke was seeking entry to her mouth, his hands squeezing her back and roving lower. She needed to put a stop to it. But just a little longer wouldn't hurt....

The blast from the truck's horn had them jumping apart like teens caught in the act. Which was exactly what Megan felt like when she looked around to find four pairs of curious eyes observing them. Her heart still racing from Luke's kiss and the fright of the blast from the horn, she said, "I don't think we should subject the children to such, uh, public displays in future, since it seems to embarrass them so much."

"I think you're the only one who's embarrassed," he said. "They're just razzing us."

"Still..."

Luke held up his hands in a gesture of surrender. "All right, if it makes you feel uncomfortable, I won't do it," he said, and strode over to his vehicle.

Feeling foolish for making such a fuss, Megan barely had time to race down the steps to kiss her son goodbye as he changed seats with Luke. Moments later, the big truck roared out of the yard, leaving dust and a suddenly bereft Megan in its wake.

Chapter Eleven

Cody decided it wasn't so bad having a father. He still didn't feel comfortable calling him "Dad," but Luke seemed cool with it. In fact, Luke seemed cool with a lot of things. And pretty uptight about others. Like his cell phone.

He'd been mad as hell his first morning in Colorado when Luke had snatched it out of his hand while he was texting Goose, one of the guys from the 'hood. Luke had confiscated it, saying he didn't want him associating with anyone from his old life. Well, how dumb was that? These were his *friends.* He didn't have anyone near his own age to talk to in Colorado—except his sisters.

That had been a big adjustment. He'd never had siblings before, never had to share his mom with anyone. He didn't realize how much he depended on her until he'd had to wait in line for her attention.

He didn't want to whine about it, though. He wasn't a baby. Not like Celeste, who in Cody's opinion demanded too much of his mom's time.

His dad had given him back his phone just before they set off on their trip to Wyoming, saying, "I've replaced your SIM card *and* got you a new number."

Cody had been furious. How was he supposed to

connect with the guys if he didn't have their numbers? And they couldn't contact him on his old number, since he had a completely new one. He'd clicked through his contacts list. It was full of O'Malley relatives' names. "In case you need to talk to anyone or you're stuck somewhere," Luke had explained with his usual abruptness.

There was no point in arguing about the fact that his father had taken away his SIM card. Cody knew he'd never get it back. He'd learned his father was really stubborn like that.

His dad had also given him a couple of driving lessons over the weekend. That had been the coolest part of moving to Colorado. He'd never imagined he'd learn how to drive. Some of the guys back in the 'hood had taught themselves to drive by stealing cars. Mostly they'd ended up smashing them—and themselves. And sometimes other guys in the car with them.

The one time Cody had accepted a ride, it had scared him so much, he'd made himself scarce whenever a heist was going down.

Anyhow, the truck his dad was teaching him on was far more powerful than any of the cars the guys had stolen in the 'hood.

Sure, his dad and he had words. But Luke never raised his voice at him. Not like the "fathers" back in the 'hood. They not only yelled at their kids, they often hit them, too.

Cody had been afraid that when he'd gotten mad at Luke over confiscating his cell phone, his dad might hit him. But he hadn't. Cody had really pushed him on that one. Called him names. The foulest names he could think of.

Luke hadn't shown any reaction. He'd just said, "That's at least a dozen contributions to the penalty box. I'll cut you some slack and call it an even ten. But next time, you'll pay the full price."

Since he'd exhausted his first week's allowance with that one infraction, Cody had been careful to mind his mouth after that.

And because he didn't have anyone he could call on his cell, Cody had rung his mom and his uncle Matt and even Daisy. Well, she'd called him. She'd wanted to know all about what he was doing, who he'd met that day, what he'd liked about the convention.

He didn't want to admit it but he really liked Daisy. She was gutsy. He thought she might be mad at him for being taken to the convention instead of her. But she was really excited for him. Cody had never had other kids get excited for him about anything.

And now they were in this fancy hotel. He'd never stayed in a hotel before. On the New Jersey trip, he and his mom had stayed in a B and B run by some old people and he'd had to keep quiet. He'd expected that he and Luke would be sharing a room. That would've been weird, though, sharing a room with someone he hardly knew. He was relieved when they'd walked up to the check-in desk and Luke had asked if they could have adjoining rooms. Luke had shown him how to unlock the doors between them. For a while there, Cody had thought Luke would insist on leaving the door between their rooms open, but he hadn't. His room was really cool. He had a king-size bed all to himself and the bathroom had free shampoo and stuff. The towels were super-soft, too. He also had a big-screen TV all to himself; he could watch pretty much whatever he wanted.

Only problem was, the first night he was so tired after the long drive, he'd fallen asleep in front of an episode of *Dog the Bounty Hunter*. His mom had never let him watch it at home.

The next night they'd had dinner with a bunch of his dad's colleagues, other ranchers. He'd never eaten such amazing food. And so much of it. And to have waiters running around at his beck and call was awesome. He'd downed so much food and so many root-beer floats that he'd fallen asleep in front of the TV again.

By day three of the convention, he'd met just about everyone there was to know in the cattle industry in the West and learned a lot. He was amazed by how much his dad knew and kinda wondered why he even needed to come to the convention, but he guessed that was what they called networking.

His dad had bought a bull to replace Orion, who was getting on in years and not impregnating as many cows as he should've been. His dad preferred what he called natural insemination rather than artificial insemination. He'd felt a bit embarrassed when Luke was talking about cows having sex, but he'd been so matter-of-fact about it that Cody's embarrassment had evaporated. He'd also learned a lot about horse-breeding. Some of the ranchers had told him his dad was known for his horses and his training. They even said he'd been on the cover of a national magazine. Cody would ask him about it when he got the chance.

When they'd first left New York, Cody hadn't wanted to believe anything good about his dad. He preferred his uncle Matt. Matt was cool. He'd been stunned to learn his uncle was the county sheriff. But when Matt had taken him on a tour of his offices and the jail as a reward for cleaning up the dishes the other night, he'd decided he liked having a sheriff in the family. Matt had even let him talk to some of the prisoners. Trusties, Uncle Matt had called them. People doing weekend detention or short-terms. The really bad guys were in a sealed-off section of the jail. He got to go into the control center where he could see everyone, but they couldn't see him. Some of the guys in there looked really tough. They looked like older versions of some of the guys he used to hang out with in his old neighborhood. That realization had brought Cody up short. No wonder his dad had been in a hurry to get him out of New York.

THE WEEK FLEW BY for Megan. Looking after three active girls was more of a handful than she'd expected, but she loved every minute of it. Even Sasha seemed to have thawed a little, particularly when she let her sleep over at Nick's house for a couple of nights. She later learned that Luke forbade sleepovers on school nights, but Megan figured that if it helped to ease the tension in the house, then she didn't see any harm.

Becky and Beth had taken over planning the wedding, saying they wanted it to be a surprise for Megan. They'd issued invitations, arranged the catering, flowers and all the minute details involved with a wedding, albeit one that was less than a week in the planning.

Their organizational skills and generosity had allowed Megan the time to look into continuing her accounting course. She was now officially enrolled in a local college and was looking forward to getting back to her studies and completing her degree.

Her paychecks from her previous employers had arrived on Wednesday, surprising Megan with their promptness—and the fact that they'd been sent at all. She smiled at the memory of Luke dealing with Jerry and Pat.

She'd taken care of her final rent and utility bills for her New York apartment. Their belongings had arrived by truck just yesterday. Now, with all the ties to her old life severed, Megan was looking forward to making a new life for Cody and herself in Colorado.

Cody called every evening to tell her about his day. He sounded as if he was having fun, meeting new people, making friends, feeling a part of the ranching community. It thrilled her to hear the enthusiasm in his voice. Her boy was back and she knew who she had to thank for it.

She'd been given driving lessons by Mrs. Robertson and Beth, been quizzed by Will on the rules of the road when he'd come to take her and the girls to his and Becky's place for dinner on two evenings.

Now, as she prepared dinner on Friday evening, waiting for Luke and Cody to get home—thankfully one day earlier than expected—Megan could see the tent erected on the lawns out back, the truck unloading chairs and tables for guests. In twenty-four hours she'd be married. Or rather, married again. Maybe the traditional ceremony would make her feel more married, more a part of Luke's life and family.

Luke's parents had arrived that morning from their cruise. Sarah and Mac O'Malley seemed excited to meet her and declared they couldn't wait to meet their grandson. Fortunately, they'd be staying with Will and Becky, meaning Megan didn't have to move out of their quarters and into Luke's bedroom. Not yet, anyway.

There was, of course, the tiny apartment over the

horse barn, but it wasn't finished yet. Jack had told her he planned on finishing it, just as soon as Matt and Beth's new home was ready for them.

She liked the way the family meshed together, pulled together, helped one another out. They were good for Cody, exactly what her son needed.

The only sour note was that she and Luke had ended up arguing on the phone two nights earlier.

Before he'd left, Luke had told her to make herself at home, familiarize herself with the organization of the ranch. On Tuesday evening, she'd wandered into his study after returning from dinner at Becky and Will's, and seen the ranch books sitting on Luke's enormous desk.

Curious to learn more about the running of the ranch, she'd sat in his worn leather office chair, propped her feet on the desk and started going through the books, hoping to be able to help Luke with the accounting. She remembered Gil McIntyre's reaction when Luke told him she was studying accounting. His sudden change of demeanor, slight though it was, bothered her even now.

It didn't take Megan long to realize something was amiss. According to the checkbook and the printout of his bank records, Luke had made out large checks to a particular vendor, yet a quick search of the internet didn't bring up any reference to this vendor—All Western States Supply, Inc.

What sort of company could trade so heavily in ranch supplies, but not have a presence or a reference to it anywhere on the internet? It was too late to call Luke to see if he knew the vendor. One pervading fear filled her mind as she tried to sleep: How deeply was Luke involved in what appeared to be a dummy company?

Not until the following afternoon did Megan have a chance to get back to the ranch books and do some cross-checking. She dreaded finding out that Luke was a cheat, but from everything she knew of him, it just didn't sit right.

Heart racing, she searched back through his bank records, until finally, eighteen months earlier, they reconciled perfectly. What had happened a year and a half ago?

And then she found it. The hair stood up on the back of her neck. Luke had changed accountants, from a firm that had handled the ranch's business for many years, to Gil McIntyre.

But why change to Gil? Simply because he was a friend? Because he'd found the anomaly that resulted in a tax refund? For all Megan knew, Gil could have been responsible for the anomaly in the first place.

Suspecting that Gil, based on his reaction to Luke's news that she was studying to be an accountant, was somehow involved in the dummy company, Megan called the companies that had previoulsy supplied the ranch. After asking their current prices on the goods he'd ordered, she did some quick calculations on the difference between their quoted prices and what Luke was paying All Western States Supply, Inc. He was paying at least ten percent over listed prices. But why? Just because All Western bundled the invoices into one, therefore saving a little time with checkwriting?

She then called the companies back and asked if they'd heard of or provided equipment and supplies to All Western. Many had, and they weren't happy about it.

They'd received payments months after they'd sent out their goods. She asked if any supplied to Two Elk Ranch in Peaks County. They did, and none of them could understand why Luke and many of the other ranchers in the area had changed to this new billing system with All Western.

After thanking them and hanging up, Megan sat back and let out her breath. According to the checkbook, Luke had paid All Western immediately upon receipt of the goods, not months later.

If, as she suspected, Gil was skimming money off the top for supplying to the ranches now in his dummy company's network, it could amount to hundreds of thousands—possibly millions—of dollars.

Everything pointed to the fact that Luke was being embezzled by his so-called friend and he seemed to have no idea.

She checked and rechecked her figures and then, hands shaking, she'd called Luke.

After quickly explaining what she'd discovered, she waited for Luke's reaction. It was far from what she'd expected.

After a long moment, he said one word. "Megan."

In the way he said her name, she could hear the frustration and something that sounded like anger in his voice. "This is none of your business!"

Taken aback, Megan reminded him, "You told me to familiarize myself with the ranch organization. I assumed, perhaps foolishly, that you were referring to the *financial* organization."

When he didn't respond, Megan said, "Then you're aware of what's going on?" Surely Luke wasn't party to this fraud! Surely he wasn't cheating his parents and brothers out of their share of the ranch profits?

"It doesn't matter what I'm aware of. I didn't give you permission to go snooping around and accusing an old friend of cheating me."

Megan could feel her own anger rising. "You made it my business!" she said. Feeling she needed to remind him, she repeated, "You told me to make myself at home, familiarize myself with how the business is run."

"You have no qualifications."

"Luke, I'm studying to be an accountant," she pointed out unnecessarily, needing to hammer the fact home.

"Like I said, you have no qualifications."

"I have more than you! And even a halfwit could tell that something fishy's going on here," she countered, furious at his patronizing remarks.

"Are you implying that I'm cheating on my taxes?"

Megan's pause before answering had him snapping at her. "Thanks! Nice to know my *wife* doesn't trust me."

"Oh, for heaven's sake, Luke, what was I supposed to think when I looked at the books?"

"I trust Gil McIntyre implicitly. He found an error our previous CPA made in filing the ranch's tax returns with the IRS. He's not only a friend, he was working at the firm at the time and offered to file an amended return for the previous year on our behalf, which resulted in a huge refund. Gil went into business for himself soon after and I followed him there."

Just as Megan suspected. How convenient for Gil to start up his own firm soon after finding the anomaly that had resulted in the tax refund. She was already wondering how many other clients of the original firm had also been contacted by Gil about a similar anomaly in their taxes and how many had followed him to his new business.

As she was about to suggest this to Luke, he said, "I trust Gil. Do you understand that? This has nothing to do with you. So butt out!"

Megan felt as though she'd been slapped in the face, but she worked at keeping her voice calm. "Don't speak to me like that, Luke. Gil McIntyre is cheating you! But if you're okay with that, then fine."

Before he could say anything more, before she burst into tears at the harshness of Luke's tone, she hung up.

He called back immediately but she let it go to voice mail. Right now, she needed a long, hot soak in the tub. She was doing her driver's test the next morning and needed to put Luke out of her mind.

SHE'D SAILED THROUGH the test and that evening had told Cody the details. She took her test on Thursday at the Department of Motor Vehicles in Silver Springs. She'd been nervous but had passed without any trouble. Her son sounded so proud of her that her spirits lifted as he told her all about a bull they'd purchased to replace Orion.

"And Luke said to tell you we'll be home tomorrow night instead of Saturday."

As they said their goodbyes, Megan thought, *Luke couldn't find the time to tell me himself?*

She played back Luke's message from the night before, but all he'd said was he didn't appreciate her hanging up on him and that they'd talk about it when he got home.

Didn't appreciate? Well, she didn't appreciate him being so nasty when all she was doing was trying to help. Feeling perverse, she decided to work on the ranch books some more, make notes about the anomalies and get them in proper order. Maybe the physical proof of the figures being embezzled from the ranch accounts would prove to Luke what was going on. She was almost tempted to pay a visit to Gil McIntyre and ask him what he was up to, but decided against it. She'd noticed the accountant's name and his wife's on the wedding invitation list. The reception wasn't the time or place to confront him, either. Better for her to gather evidence of the dummy company's trading, lay everything out for Luke and for him to take whatever action he felt necessary.

THE SOUND OF THE TRUCK'S horn had Megan racing to the front door and onto the veranda. She waited there, taking in the scene as they drove up, her son leaping from the truck and striding toward her. "Mom!" he cried, and caught her in a huge bear hug. "I've missed you," he said, and released her.

"I've missed you, too, honey," she said, stroking his hair. His newly shorn hair. And, to her relief, the piercings were gone. All that remained was a neat hole in his lip that she hoped would soon heal over. "I swear you've grown a foot in the past week," she said, stepping back but still holding his hands, unwilling to let go of him just yet.

What a difference a week had made.

He seemed to have filled out. As if he'd eaten well and gotten some exercise. And he was tanned. The resemblance between him and his father was uncanny.

"It's only been five days, Mom. I can't have grown during that time," he protested. He hugged her again and said, "I've gotta help Dad with getting the new bull settled. You should see him, Mom. He's magnificent. The ladies will be very happy to make his acquaintance, I'm sure!"

"Naughty boy!" she admonished, gently slapping his shoulder and watching him return to the truck. *Dad.* He'd called his father "Dad."

She watched Luke, surrounded by his daughters, all of them vying for his attention. He hugged each one close, kissed them. They obviously objected to his five-o'clock shadow as each one wiped her cheek with a disgusted expression.

They eventually dragged themselves away to welcome Cody home, leaving Luke alone by the truck.

Megan willed him to look at her. And he did. His gaze sent desire and want and need humming through her veins. Silently she begged him to open his arms, invite her in, tell her it was okay, that their fight didn't mean anything. But he didn't. Instead, he stood there staring at her, as if waiting for her to make the first move. Suddenly Megan didn't feel so sure of herself. What if she ran down the veranda and into his arms but he turned away? She'd feel like a fool. Totally rejected.

She tried to make her feet move, but they wouldn't. She willed Luke to come to her instead, take her in his arms and kiss her like he never wanted to stop. Say that everything was okay. Apologize for being a jerk. But he stayed where he was.

It was as though a wide, wild river divided them and they were each unable to leap into the treacherous waters....

Finally, Luke turned away and went to help Cody unload the bull. Megan pressed her lips together to prevent them from trembling as she returned to the kitchen. But the sight of the huge tent the caterers had set up made her stomach roil. What was she thinking? Luke didn't love her, didn't want her. He'd admitted he was only going through with this farce of a wedding ceremony for his family.

That implied he sure didn't want it. She fought the tears that threatened at the realization that she was so redundant around here. Luke had saved their son from street gangs and juvenile detention. Luke had a family who loved him, cared about him. She had no one but Cody and, judging by the way he was calling his father "Dad," she probably didn't really have him anymore, either. Her son's world had expanded, which she knew was a good thing, but it seemed to leave her without a role.

She made an effort to suppress her feelings of worthlessness, of being unwanted, but they overwhelmed her, welled up and threatened to suffocate her. She fled to her room, needing a sanctuary, somewhere she could cry long and loud, to rail against the injustice. She hated giving in to self-pity, but she felt so afraid. Afraid she was unworthy of being loved....

BY THE TIME SHE MADE IT to her room, sanity had prevailed. The O'Malleys—the whole family, including Luke's parents—were coming for dinner in less than half an hour.

She couldn't greet her future in-laws looking as if she'd gone ten rounds in a boxing ring. So she splashed her face with cold water and went into the kitchen to make sure the Beef Stroganoff Becky had designated as Megan's contribution to the meal wasn't burning. Becky would be bringing salads and potatoes au gratin, Beth the dessert, Jack chocolates and the mysterious Adam had elected to bring appetizers. Becky had intimated to Megan that she didn't trust him to bring anything more substantial than a bowl of olives from the supermarket deli, so she was fixing some crackers and dips.

Megan was looking forward to meeting Luke's youngest brother. All she knew of him was that he was a firefighter and lived in Boulder. He seemed to be a bit of a recluse.

"Hey, there!"

Megan spun around, startled out of her musings by Becky's enthusiastic greeting. Becky had her hands full, so she leaned toward Megan over the potato dish and kissed her cheek.

"That smells divine," Megan said, taking the dish from her and placing it beside the oven.

"One of Will's favorites. Mind you, he declares anything I make his favorite, so you can't count on him to be discerning."

Will arrived loaded down with a basket containing salads on one arm and his baby daughter, Lily, in the other.

She held out her hands to Megan, who gladly took her from Will. She and Lily had become friends over the past week, having spent several days together while Becky planned the wedding or they shopped together.

Soon the kitchen was full of O'Malleys and the noise level was rising in proportion to the number of people showing up, laden with food.

Thankfully, Sarah took over, directing her sons and

grandchildren to set the outdoor tables and take the food outside.

Last to arrive was Adam. He was as dark-featured and well-muscled as Luke, perhaps a little shorter. He shook Megan's hand, his grip firm.

"We meet at last," were the first words to pop out of Megan's mouth.

Adam nodded but she sensed he was sizing her up. Searching for any flaws in her character. It was unsettling, since he hadn't actually returned her greeting.

"Neanderthal!" Will said, lightly clipping his brother on the back of the head. "Say hello to your new sister-in-law."

"Hello," he said obediently, and then he smiled and it lit up the room. "I'm pleased to meet you at last, too, Megan."

From then on, the evening went well. So well that Megan almost forgot how upset she still was with Luke. But she was soon reminded of it once everyone had left for home and the children had been put to bed.

She was coming downstairs from tucking Celeste in when Luke appeared out of the shadows, grabbed her hand and led her into the study.

He closed the door, dropped her hand and crossed his arms, demanding, "Just what are you accusing Gil of doing?"

So Megan repeated what she knew, showed him the anomalies she'd found, but felt as if she was talking to a brick wall. Luke's loyalties lay with Gil, because of their shared past and because of some stupid tax refund! For all they knew, Gil might have purposely made the mistake under someone else's name, then "discovered" it and wormed his way into Luke's confidence by refiling the return and gaining him the refund.

If she had time, she could probably trace it all the way back to when Gil worked for the other firm. See who'd really filled out the forms incorrectly in the first place. But she didn't have time; all she had was one angry husband who trusted some shyster more than he trusted her.

They had a terrible argument and, in the end, Megan had said, "Check the books again, Luke. Check the notes I've made. I'm not wrong!" Then she yanked open the door, walked outside and pulled it shut with more force than necessary.

LUKE SMASHED HIS PILLOW, trying to get it into a more comfortable shape. But he knew it wasn't the pillow causing his restlessness. He'd been unfair to Megan. Downright patronizing, in fact. What if she was right about Gil? What if he had committed fraud?

Luke had been too stubborn to believe her and too dog-tired to check the books or read Megan's copious notes before turning in. He'd needed to get some sleep before their wedding.

Now he regretted it because the same thing kept playing in his mind—the fact that he'd handed over much of the bookkeeping to Gil once he'd appointed him as the ranch accountant. Luke had tried to keep his own accounts but it had never been one of his strong points and when Gil had found a company that would provide many of his supplies, Luke had been happy to write them checks, based on the monthly invoices that came via Gil.

Maybe he should've taken a closer look at that company a long time ago.

He kicked back the covers, determined to go and apologize to Megan—whether she was right or wrong. Then the time on the bedside clock caught his eye. Two-fifteen. Megan probably wouldn't appreciate having her sleep interrupted, no matter how contrite he was. It would have to wait until morning.

MEGAN'S TEARS WERE FINALLY spent sometime after midnight. Coming to the ranch had caused so many of the old hurts of her childhood to resurface. She'd thought by cutting off all contact with her family that she could put those childhood demons to rest. And she had. For a long while.

But now those feelings of not being good enough, not being wanted, were back.

At one point during their discussion, Luke had gone ballistic. He'd repeated that he trusted Gil. Told her again that she wasn't qualified. She felt so completely alone. Where had the attentive husband of last weekend gone? The gentle lover who'd seduced her in a meadow on a carpet of wildflowers?

The past week she'd been on an emotional roller coaster and it didn't look as if the ride was going to end anytime soon.

She felt like death warmed over, emotionally and physically exhausted. She was going to look like hell in the morning. Not that it mattered. She wouldn't be walking up the aisle at precisely 11:00 a.m.

Megan wasn't really certain where she might be, but she wouldn't be saying her "I do's" to Luke. Not after the way he'd treated her. She'd been more contented before he came back into her life and tried to take it over, turned it upside down, causing bad memories to resurface....

LUKE ROSE EARLY and went to check on his horses. He was half hoping to find Megan in the kitchen, having an early-morning cup of coffee, but the house was silent. He strode out into the yard and headed for the barn. It was a beautiful day, not a cloud in the sky. A good day to get married.

He smiled to himself. He was looking forward to marrying Megan in front of his family and friends. Their first ceremony had been too abrupt, forced on them by Cody. He probably should've put his foot down then and there, but he didn't know Cody well enough. All he saw was a defiant punk of a kid who swore he'd rather go to juvenile detention than Colorado if Luke didn't marry his mother on the spot.

They'd both been thoroughly manipulated by Cody, but Luke had to admit he was grateful for Cody's stand. Who knew where they might be today if they weren't married?

The only problem was, he and Megan hadn't been living like husband and wife. Would that change tonight? On their honeymoon?

He'd changed his mind about going somewhere local and had instead chosen somewhere special for them to spend the night on their way to the airport in Denver and their final destination in the Florida Keys. There was a spa hotel in Boulder that offered pampering for its guests. He'd booked a couple's massage for when they arrived later this afternoon, hoping that would help

Megan relax, followed by a romantic dinner in their suite.

He'd pretty much scheduled everything—except his apology.

MEGAN SLEPT UNTIL AFTER eight and was awakened by Sasha bringing her coffee and a bagel. Soon, her room was full of children, with Daisy lounging on the end of the bed, Celeste under the covers with her and Cody sprawled in the bedroom chair.

It was comforting being surrounded by her children. Only Luke was missing from the picture. Maybe he'd be missing forever if they couldn't resolve their differences before the wedding. Her heart had thawed a little toward him during the night. He was used to being in control of his ranch, but there was one aspect he'd handed over to someone else; maybe he'd realized by now that he'd made a mistake. It would be hard for him to admit he'd been embezzled and had failed to notice it until Megan's discovery. Luke was a proud man. Perhaps she hadn't approached him in the right way....

"Mommy?"

Celeste's questioning voice woke Megan from her musings. "What's up, pumpkin?"

"Are you mad at me?"

Megan smiled and hugged Celeste. "How could anyone be angry with a gorgeous little dumpling like you?" She kissed the top of Celeste's fair head.

"You look tired," Sasha said in her usual direct manner.

"I didn't sleep very well," Megan admitted, determined not to rise to Sasha's bait.

"Your eyes are all puffy," Daisy told her. "Have you been crying? My eyes always get puffy when I cry."

Daisy's admission surprised Megan. She, of all the girls, always seemed so composed, not prone to emotional outbursts. Maybe she didn't know Daisy as well as she thought she did. Maybe she should plan a mother-daughter day just for her and Daisy.

She threw back the covers and climbed out of bed. "I need to take a shower and you girls need to get ready for the hairstylist Aunt Becky booked to come and do your hair."

That was all the motivation Celeste needed. She bounded off the bed and dashed out the door. There was nothing that little girl liked more than having her hair done.

Cody unwound himself from the chair and muttered, "Girl stuff, ugh," and left the room, followed by Daisy, who no doubt felt the same way.

Sasha seemed inclined to linger. Megan guessed she had something on her mind.

"What can I do for you, Sasha?"

The girl picked up the breakfast tray and held it in front of her. "Are you sure you want to marry my dad?"

"We're already married, Sasha," Megan reminded her in an even voice. "The ceremony today is for the benefit of your father's family and friends."

"Yes, but—"

Megan sank onto the edge of the bed and patted the spot beside her.

For a moment, she feared the girl would ignore her, but with a huff Sasha placed the tray on the nightstand and sat down.

Megan angled herself toward Sasha. If this was any other child, she'd have clasped her hands, but not Sasha. She was far too brittle, too prickly.

"Sasha, I know you don't like me very much. And whether you want to like someone or not is entirely your choice." She noticed the girl squirming. Obviously, she didn't like being called on her attitude. Well, tough. They needed to clear the air.

"I know you were upset to suddenly get a brother and stepmother dumped on you. Believe me, when I woke up last Friday I didn't expect that by the end of the day, I'd have a husband and three stepdaughters."

Apparently, Sasha had never thought of what a shock her changed family circumstances must've been for Megan, and a smile quivered on the edges of her mouth.

Megan smiled, too, trying to break the tension further. "So what I'm trying to say is this. If you have a problem with me, please don't sulk about it or make unkind remarks. Just talk to me about your feelings and we'll see if we can find some common ground."

Sasha didn't say anything for he longest time, and then finally she looked Megan directly in the eye and said, "Do you love my dad?"

Megan hadn't been prepared for that question but she answered it honestly. She shrugged. "I do have…feelings for him. But adult relationships are so…complicated."

"Tell me about it!" Sasha said with a sigh. "I heard you and Daddy fighting last night."

Oh, dear. Megan hadn't realized their voices were so loud. She'd remember that in future. "We weren't fighting. We were having a disagreement."

"There's a difference?"

"Like I said, adult relationships are complicated."

"What were you disagreeing about?"

Megan stood. "That's between your father and me for the moment. But I plan on getting it resolved as soon as possible. And I can't do that until I've had a shower and freshened up."

Sasha took that as her cue and picked up the tray again. She walked to the door, then stopped and looked at her. "Thanks for talking to me," she said.

Taken aback, Megan said, "You're welcome. I'm glad we talked too, Sasha."

MEGAN STEPPED UNDER the shower and let the cool water wash over her face. She'd glimpsed herself in the bathroom mirror and been shocked at how puffy her eyes were. All the more reason to do what she intended to do before walking down the aisle today. Because, yes, she'd decided she *was* going through with the ceremony.

Twenty minutes later, dressed in jeans and a T-shirt, she walked into Luke's study, left a note on his desk and collected the ranch books. She drove into town, found a store that did photocopying and, another twenty minutes later, she had triplicate copies of the accounts. After posting one copy to Matt with a note explaining the reason for sending them to him, she called Gil McIntyre's office and arranged to meet him there, telling him she'd be coming into money and needed some advice on investing it.

Gil had said he'd be more than happy to meet her. However, he wasn't quite so happy when he saw what she pulled out of her bag.

"What are you doing with those?" he demanded, his earlier affability evaporating.

"I just have a few things I want clarified, Gil, if you have the time."

Suddenly Gil seemed to realize that Megan was due to tie the knot in less than an hour. "I have the time, but you don't. Shouldn't you be getting all prettied up?" he said, indicating her casual outfit.

"I should be, Gil, but you see, there's a little matter of the argument my groom and I had last night regarding how you'd been 'taking care' of the ranch's financial matters."

"What do you mean?" he snarled.

Megan noted how quickly his manner changed. "I think you know exactly what I mean. As Luke mentioned when we met, I'm studying to become an accountant, so while he was away this past week, I went through the books. What I discovered is that you, posing as a dummy corporation, have been helping yourself to quite a lot of the ranch's profits."

"You can't prove that."

"Yes. I can," Megan said in as reasonable a voice as she could manage. She saw his hand slip beneath the desk as he opened a drawer. The way he kept his eyes on her was unsettling. Maybe she'd bitten off more than she could chew?

"Not if you're dead and the books are nowhere to be found," he said calmly, bringing a handgun out of the drawer and training it on her.

Megan felt her insides turn to water. This was the last thing she'd expected. She cursed her naiveté. *Then why did you make those copies and send one to Matt?* a little voice demanded.

"Put that away!" she said, desperate to keep the fear out of her voice. Gil McIntyre was a cheat and a bully, and she had to let him know who was in control. "I'm asking you to explain these anomalies. You don't need a gun to do that."

Gil raised the weapon, gesturing that she should stand. *So much for acting tough,* she thought, and rose slowly to her feet.

Gil rose, too, and came around the desk. He reminded her of some B-grade movie gangster, the way he held the weapon, standing far too close to her.

He angled the gun toward the door and said, "Move."

Chapter Twelve

"What the hell did you say to her?" Matt almost roared.

"Goodness! What *is* all this noise?" Sarah demanded as she bustled into the kitchen, followed by Will, Jack and Adam. All the brothers were dressed in tuxedos. Each looked as uncomfortable as the others.

"He scared Megan off," Matt said, his eyes never leaving Luke's face.

"*What?*" Sarah steered her two warring sons away from the kitchen—and the sudden interest the caterers were showing in their conversation.

They all ended up in the living room, where Becky and Beth were fussing over the girls' bridesmaid dresses.

Sarah turned and asked Matt, "What do you mean, he scared Megan off?"

"No one can find her anywhere. Luke thinks she took off like Tory did."

"On her *wedding* day?" Will said. "Don't be ridiculous! Even Tory needed longer than that to figure out what a grumpy pain in the a—"

"Will!" Becky snapped. She indicated the children. Celeste's lower lip was trembling.

"Where's my mommy? I want my mommy!" she cried.

"Well done, you two." Beth lifted Celeste onto her hip. "Go take your squabbles somewhere else," she said, heading for the stairs, Celeste sobbing into her shoulder. She turned back, her face thunderous. "Go and find her and don't come back until you do!"

They all stared after her, surprised by Beth's outburst. She was usually the most unflappable of all of them.

Daisy crossed her arms and fixed her father with a glare. "So what have you done wrong *this* time?"

"Go to your room!"

"No!" Daisy defied her father's command. "I'm stayin' right here till you tell me what you and Uncle Matt were fightin' about."

Luke sighed. "We don't know where Megan is," he explained. "Any ideas?"

"Has this got anything to do with that fight you two had last night?"

Luke felt his face warm with embarrassment. He hadn't realized he'd raised his voice that much. Daisy wasn't one to be fobbed off with lies. "Probably," he admitted.

Daisy nodded.

"She wouldn't have gone anywhere without Cody," Sash pointed out.

"She's right," Will said. "And Cody's out back with Pop."

"No, I'm not. What's going on?" Cody asked as he joined them.

"Have you seen your mother?"

"Not since breakfast. Why? What's going on?" he repeated.

"We can't find your mom," Matt said.

Cody's eyes narrowed. "Does this have anything to do with the fight I heard you two having last night?" he demanded of Luke.

"Yes!" everyone else answered for him.

"Have you checked your phone messages?" Cody suggested.

Luke hurried into the study to retrieve his cell phone. He'd left it in a drawer, not wanting to be disturbed by ranch business today. But the first thing he noticed was that the ranch books he'd left on the desk were missing and in their place was a note. Sure enough, it was from Megan. His heart chilled as he read it.

"Is it from Mom?"

"Yeah."

"Can I see?" Will asked.

Luke handed it over to Will, who read it, then looked up at Luke. "She sounds pretty pissed with you. Are you sure you want to go after her?"

"Of course I do, dammit!"

Matt snatched the note out of Will's hand, read it and returned it to Luke. "What exactly happened last night?"

"None of your business," Luke muttered.

Matt crossed his arms. "Okay, so you had a fight. At any point in the past week, did you tell Megan you loved her?"

Luke ceased pacing and frowned. "No. But I married her, didn't I?"

Matt's snort of derision had Luke's head coming up.

"You married Tory and you clearly weren't in love with her. What sort of message do you think that conveyed to Megan?" He paused and considered his words. "You *have* told her the truth about Tory, haven't you?"

Luke shook his head. "Not all of it. I didn't want to criticize the mother of my daughters."

Matt snorted again. "You idiot! Forget Tory. Megan is something else again. That woman didn't trick you into marrying her. Instead, she kept Cody's existence a secret because she believed you were married—which by then you were—and didn't want to cause any problems for you. She married you to keep her son out of juvenile detention and probably believes that's the only reason you married her—because you were *forced* to."

"She's the only honorable person in this whole mess and you're a fool!" Will burst out. "Quite frankly, I can't blame her for leaving. You don't deserve her."

"Where's my mom?" Cody tore the note from Luke's grasp. He read it aloud as everyone crowded around him. "'Gone to see Gil McIntyre. When I've proved I'm right, maybe you'll trust me. I'm not marrying you until you do. M.' Who's Gil McIntyre?" Cody demanded.

"The ranch accountant," Sarah answered, and crossed her arms. "What is going on, Luke?"

He quickly outlined the gist of his conversation with Megan the night before. "Her accusations were so outrageous, I told her to mind her own business."

Will crossed his arms, too. "Gee, the O'Malley charm gene sure missed you."

"Will!" his mother admonished. "This is serious." She turned to her eldest son. "Luke, could her concerns have any foundation?"

"I didn't think so at the time, but I looked at everything this morning and I suspect she might be right. I need someone independent, a qualified CPA, to take a look."

"But Megan's studying to be an accountant," Will put in. "She must have a grasp of these things."

"I didn't see how she could just come in here, read a few figures and deduce that we're being embezzled. She's not a qualified accountant yet and—"

"Neither are you!" Matt and Will roared together.

Sarah covered her ears. "Goodness! This is worse than when you were all in high school."

Jack, ever the peacemaker, put his arm around his mom. "Maybe you should take a seat. All this excitement isn't good for your heart."

"There's nothing wrong with my heart. But there's definitely something wrong with your blockhead of a brother!" Her blue eyes bored into Luke's. "No wonder she's gone off to prove herself. Go and find her and apologize for your incredible stupidity!" she roared.

Luke flinched at the harshness of his mother's words. And the volume. His mom rarely lost her temper, but right now she looked ready to explode.

He punched Megan's number into his cell phone, but it went straight to voice mail. He speed-dialed Gil's office number, but it merely rang.

He shrugged. "No answer. She's probably on her way back here."

"And if she isn't?" Matt said. "Think about it. If she's accused him of embezzling money from the ranch, and she's taken the books with her to prove it, she could be putting herself in a very dangerous position. Embezzlement is a serious crime, but if Gil disposed of Megan, and the books, then there wouldn't be any evidence."

"Disposed?" Cody's query had them all turning to

him as if they'd forgotten he was there. "You mean he might *kill* my mom?"

"Daddy?" Sasha's eyes were filled with tears. "You've gotta go save her!"

Sarah ushered Daisy and Sasha from the room. Once that was done, she whirled on Luke.

"For heaven's sake, Megan's raised your son alone for over fourteen years. In spite of all her family's objections, she refused to have an abortion or give him away. She needs you, Luke. *Go and find her!*"

Becky strode out of the room, but when Luke's cell rang, she raced back in as he answered it, hitting the speaker button so everyone could listen in.

"Megan? Are you all right?" he asked, not caring how desperate he sounded. "Where are you, honey?"

He waited impatiently for her to answer, but it was Gil he heard. Luke barely recognized his voice. "I'm here, *honey*," he teased.

"Where's Megan?" Luke demanded. "Put her on."

"Not so fast! I want you to know how it feels to have something you want taken away from you," Gil said.

"What are you talking about?" Luke demanded.

"Tory."

"*Tory?* What the hell do you mean?"

"I wanted her so badly—but she was only interested in you."

"And that's my fault?"

"You got her pregnant. After that, I never had a chance."

"Trust me, Gil. I did you a favor."

"Not the way I see it. Tory and I could've had a great life together, Instead I ended up with Betsy." Luke could hear the snarl in his voice.

"Betsy's a good woman, Gil," he said evenly. "You're a lucky man."

"I didn't want a good woman! I wanted one who knew her way around the bedroom."

Luke didn't know what to say to that. He seemed to be inflaming the situation by arguing. "Gil, I don't want to fight with you. Let me talk to Megan. Please."

"I guess I can allow you two lovebirds to have one final conversation," he said, and Luke could feel his contempt.

"Luke?"

Relief flooded him at hearing Megan's voice. But she sounded terrified.

Matt had called the sheriff's department to have someone drop by Gil's office and his home, and he'd just shaken his head to indicate they hadn't found him or Megan at either location.

"Where are you, Megan?"

"I…can't tell you. But I haven't been this scared since our first date. Lu—"

Megan's voice was cut off as Gil came back on. "I hope you enjoyed your final conversation with your wife, O'Malley." The phone went dead.

"Where is she?" everyone shouted as Luke looked up.

"Did she give you any sign of where she might be?" Matt asked.

Luke shook his head. "She only said she hadn't been this scared since our first date."

"Where did you take her?" Matt asked impatiently.

It was then that Luke realized Megan had been giving him a message. He started toward the front door. "For a picnic at Inspiration Point. I'll bet that's where he's got her!"

He was halfway to his car before Matt and the others caught up with him. "We'll take my vehicle," Matt said.

"No." Luke climbed into his big SUV. "You drive too slowly and I don't want to alert him with sirens." He started the car as Jack, Adam and Will climbed into the backseat.

Matt took the front passenger seat, pulled out his cell phone and dispatched vehicles to Inspiration Point, warning them not to use their sirens.

"Dad?"

Luke had been about to step on the gas, when his son's plea halted his foot. Cody had never called him "Dad" to his face before. It was a watershed moment in their relationship.

"Hop in, son," he said, his voice hoarse with emotion.

Will climbed over into the third row of seats, making room for Cody.

The SUV tore out of the gates of Two Elk, narrowly missing Frank and Edna Farquar in their enormous Caddy. Frank's pet pig, Louella, and Charles, their dog, had their heads stuck out either side of the Caddy's rear windows.

"Inspiration Point?" Matt echoed. "That makes sense when you think about it. One-thousand-foot cliffs straight to the valley floor."

"Do you mind?" Luke growled, jerking his head at Cody sitting behind them. His gut twisted at a terrifying vision of Megan falling over the cliff she feared so much. He stepped harder on the gas, the needle passing seventy as he took the turns in the road, crossing to the other side.

"Easy, Luke!" Matt warned.

"Get out if you don't like the way I drive," Luke told him through clenched teeth. In his rearview mirror, he saw his brothers and Cody checking their seat belts.

"SO, HERE WE ARE." Gil cut the connection and tossed Megan's cell over the cliff. She swallowed as she imagined him dispatching her as easily. "Just you and me."

Megan prayed that Luke would understand her cryptic remark about the location of their first date. But in case he didn't, she had some fast talking to do.

Raising her hands in a gesture of surrender, she said, "Look, how about if we forget this conversation ever happened? Luke said I should've minded my own business and that I wasn't qualified, that I didn't know what I was talking about. Maybe I made a mistake…."

"Too late. You've sown doubt in his mind. He'll come looking for me…and you. Only he won't find me because I'll be on the next plane to the Cayman Islands. But he *will* find you—or at least what's left of you—at the bottom of this cliff." He grabbed her arms and hauled her closer to the edge and glanced over.

Megan could feel her head spinning. Praying Luke would understand her cryptic clue, she stalled for time.

"Take me with you!" she said rashly. "Take me away from this hick town and that king of hicks, Luke O'Malley."

That got Gil's attention and he released his grip on her arm a little. "I thought you were looking forward to getting married today."

Megan gave an exaggerated snort. "Only for the benefit of his kids and his family. I'm just marrying him for his money, but since you've got a lot of it now, I might as well stick with you. We could have a good life together. Sun, surf…" She swallowed and added, "Sex."

Gil's eyes glittered with interest and she pressed on. "We could set up our own company down there, handling other people's finances, helping them avoid their tax burdens. We could make ourselves a nice little nest egg skimming off the top."

Gil's mouth lifted in what passed for a smile and Megan hoped she'd hooked him. "Come on. Let's get out of here," she urged, taking advantage of his momentary slip in concentration, leading him toward the car, away from the cliff edge.

They'd nearly reached his vehicle when Megan heard the sound of tires screeching on the curving road that climbed to the top of Inspiration Point. Someone was taking those bends awfully fast. Could it be Luke?

Gil must've realized it the same time she did. He dragged her toward the cliff once more. Megan fought with him, trying to gain a foothold on the gravelly surface.

"You bitch!" Gil screamed. "You tried to trick me!"

"No! Please don't do this," Megan begged as she was dragged ever closer to the precipice. She debated trying to turn the tables and shove him over, hoping to somehow escape his grasp. But she was no match for Gil's strength as he hauled her to the edge, then spun her around so that only the tips of her toes were in contact with the ground.

Megan squeezed her eyes shut, offering up a silent

prayer that her death would be fast and merciful. And then her stomach rose to her throat as he shoved her backward over the cliff.

"No!" LUKE CRIED as his vehicle crested the last bend onto the top of the cliff.

Everything seemed to happen in slow motion as he saw Gil shove Megan off Inspiration Point and then run to his car.

Luke spent a fraction of a second debating as to whether he should chase Gil or go after Megan—although he was sure there was nothing he could do to save her now.

"Leave him," Matt growled beside him. "There's only one way down and I have deputies coming up." He called them, telling them to apprehend Gil McIntyre, adding a description of his car.

Luke pulled up beside the cliff face and was out of his vehicle and peering over the edge before the dust had settled.

The dust stung his eyes and he wiped them impatiently. Heart pounding with fear, he tore off his tux jacket and sprawled on his stomach to get a better view, dreading what he'd see.

Thirty feet down he spotted a piece of blue fabric blowing in the breeze. He eased his body closer to the precipice.

"Whoa there!" Adam warned, holding his feet.

"I can see something!" Luke shouted. "Let me get closer."

"Better not to look," Adam said.

Luke ignored him, edging forward so he hung over

the cliff, aware of other hands reaching out to steady him. And that was when he saw her.

He scrambled backward and turned to his brothers. "Get me some rope. She's about thirty feet down on a narrow ledge. I have to get to her."

Will started off to get rope from the back of the SUV, but Matt stayed him with a hand on his shoulder. "That's too risky, Luke. Wait until mountain rescue gets here." He put a call through to his office.

"That could take too long," Luke protested. "The ledge is so narrow that if she moves even a couple of inches, she'll go over the side." He took the rope from Will, who'd ignored Matt and retrieved the coil that was always kept in their ranch vehicles, and began to fasten it around his waist.

Adam stayed his hand. "Let me go. I'm trained in rescue."

Luke pulled out of his grasp. "No! It's too dangerous. I got her into this mess and I'm going to get her out of it."

"Luke..." Matt warned.

"Look, you either help me or get the hell out of here!" Luke exploded, in no mood for Matt's cautious ways.

Shaking his head, Matt took the end of the rope and looped it onto the SUV's tow bar as Adam tied it around himself to belay the rope out to Luke. "Be careful," he warned as Luke stepped off the cliff edge. Within moments, he'd lost sight of his brother altogether.

Matt turned away and noticed Cody, white-faced with fear, staring at the place he'd last seen his father. He strode over to the boy and put an arm around his shoulders. "Your mom will be fine," he said, not knowing if it was truth or lie, but needing to comfort his nephew.

No doubt Cody was thinking that if anything happened to Luke, he could well lose both his parents on the same day.

Jack, equally white-faced, set a hand on Cody's shoulder and said, "I'll take care of Cody. You'll need to help to coordinate the rescue effort and I have no experience with that."

Grateful to have Jack take over, Matt clapped him on the back and said, "Thanks," then returned to the cliff edge.

Will was lying flat on his stomach, calling directions to Adam about how much rope to let out. "Easy. Easy," he said. "He's almost there."

LUKE CONCENTRATED ON HIS footing, thankful that someone as powerful as Adam was on the other end of the rope, playing it out. He could hear Will clearly, giving directions as he was lowered to the narrow ledge Megan was lying on. He signaled to Will that he was stepping to the side to get around her. Once he was past, he stepped back and dropped down a little more so he was level with her head, his feet braced against the rock face. He indicated that Adam should stop playing out the rope.

There was no room on the shelf for him, but this position, however precarious, gave him some sense of safety, some reassurance that should Megan fall, he might be able to catch her.

She was lying on her stomach, her head facing toward him, her eyes closed. A small pool of blood was forming beneath her head.

"Megan," he whispered.

She didn't move.

"Sweetheart. I'm here. Can you open your eyes?"

Still nothing. Luke feared the worst. He was reluctant to feel for her pulse, knowing that if he found none, there would be no hope for her.

"Is she alive?" Matt shouted from above him, leaving Luke no choice but to reach out and place two fingers against Megan's throat. But his hands shook too fiercely, so he cupped a hand over her mouth and nose.

Relief filled him as he felt her breath against his palm.

Megan moaned and opened her eyes.

He could feel the biggest grin in the world splitting his face.

"Luke?"

She tried to lift her head and look around but Luke cautioned her. "Don't move, honey. We'll get you out of here as soon as we can."

"Out?"

"Rescue teams are on their way."

"Rescue? What? Where am I?"

She managed to lift her head this time, before Luke could stop her. Her eyes opened wide with fear.

And then she started to scream.

Nesting birds, disturbed by the noise, flew out of their aeries. The snapping of wings and the bird's screeching around his head caused Luke to lose his footing. He lost contact with the cliff face and dropped several feet below Megan before regaining his foothold.

"I take it she's alive," Will said with his usual irony.

Luke looked up at his brother and, for once in his life, he wasn't irritated by Will's easygoing manner. He smiled grimly and nodded his head, then alerted them to raise him a few feet.

That done, he took Megan's hand. "Honey, do you understand me when I say I don't want you to move? Not even an eyelash."

Megan stared at him wide-eyed. "How? Where?" she asked.

"You don't remember?"

Megan shook her head, loosening several pebbles from her narrow shelf.

"Just. Don't. Move," Luke warned again. "Let me talk, okay?"

Unsure what to do to make her more comfortable, he said the first words that came into his mind. "I love you, Megan. I always have."

"Don't feel you have to say things you don't mean," she mumbled.

This was good; she was talking. "Everything's going to be fine," he told her. "Help is on the way."

"Cody?" she asked.

"He's fine. He's up there waiting for you."

"I'm sorry I didn't tell you about him all those years ago."

"Shh," Luke said, soothingly. The time for Megan to apologize for anything was long past.

"MEGAN…" LUKE'S VOICE, deep but unsure, penetrated the fog of pain.

She bit down hard on her lip. She couldn't bear to let him know how much she cared, how much she hurt inside. How little pride she had left.

Her head throbbed. But the pain that tore through her

shoulder and legs was sharper. Excruciating. She closed her eyes to shut out the agony, trying to will it away.

She felt Luke's lips touch her forehead and again he whispered the words she'd wanted to hear for so long. "I love you. I always have."

Megan resisted the urge to shake herself. Instead, she opened her eyes and searched his face. Luke was an honorable man. He wouldn't lie to her about something so important, so sacred.

His voice husky with emotion, Luke asked, "Why did you leave town without saying anything all those years ago?"

She swallowed against the dryness in her throat and said, "I don't think you really want to know that."

"Of course I do."

Megan took a deep breath, then wished she hadn't as pain shot through her chest. He wanted the truth? Then he was welcome to it, in all its ugly reality. "I overheard Tory in the change room at the rec center, telling another girl about your marriage plans—"

"*What?* I wasn't going to marry Tory! We'd broken up two weeks before you came to Spruce Lake. I told you all that."

True. But when she'd overheard the conversation in the change rooms, she'd felt she had no choice except to believe what Tory was saying. "According to her, she was already pregnant when you met me, dated me…" Her voice broke. "*Slept* with me."

"She wasn't pregnant then. Nor, as it turned out, was she pregnant when I married her. Only I didn't find out the truth about that until a long time later." He sighed. "Sweetheart, we've both been victims of Tory's machinations. She told me you'd been bragging at the rec center how you'd laid a hayseed."

"You don't honestly believe I'd say something like that, do you?"

He shrugged. "At the time, yes, I'm sorry to say, I did. I was hurt and bewildered about why you'd left so suddenly. Left me in the restaurant, waiting with a huge bunch of flowers, a marriage proposal and a ring."

"What?" Megan was sure she must've been hearing things.

"I wanted to marry you, even though we'd just met. I knew you were the woman I wanted to spend the rest of my life with. Until you didn't turn up but Tory did and told me what she'd supposedly heard you say. That cut me so deeply, I can't even bear to think of it all these years later."

Megan closed her eyes and clenched her jaw, then looked back at Luke. "So what I overheard in the rec center was a setup?"

Luke nodded.

Tears filled Megan's eyes. How many years had they lost together because of the manipulations of one unhappy, obsessive woman?

"I love you." His breath whispered over her face. "I'm sorry I judged you as I judged her," he said, as if needing to convince Megan of his sincerity. "You're not Tory. You never were, you never could be. You kept Cody's existence a secret to protect me, but I didn't need protection from the truth, darlin'. I just needed you."

She swallowed the lump in her throat and said, "Don't let Tory come between us anymore."

"I won't," he vowed.

"RESCUE'S ARRIVED!" Will yelled down to them.

"We'll have you out of here in no time, sweetheart," Luke assured her. "Just stay calm and don't move."

He could hear commotion above him as rescue equipment was readied. Another head popped over the cliff face and Luke recognized the coordinator of mountain rescue for the county, Jasper Haynes.

"We'll be down in a minute. Tell her not to move."

Luke rolled his eyes and smiled at Megan.

"We need to get you up here first, Luke."

"I'm not leaving her," he called back, never breaking eye contact with Megan. "We haven't got much time right now," he said to her. "But I want you to know this. I'm sorry for being such a pigheaded fool. I'm sorry for not believing you and trusting your judgment about the ranch finances. And Gil's activities. But most of all I'm sorry I haven't allowed myself to love you the way you deserve to be loved."

She blinked away tears and he smiled. "I mean it, Megan. You're the best thing that happened to me fifteen years ago and you are now. I can't imagine my life without you and Cody in it. I hope you'll forgive me—"

He was silenced by Megan stretching out her arm and touching her finger to his bottom lip. Then her hand went limp, her eyes closed.

"Megan?"

She didn't respond. He couldn't help the fear in his voice as he called up to Jasper. "She's passed out! Get down here *now!*"

The words had barely left his mouth when a rescue litter appeared over the side, along with two rescue personnel in harnesses.

Bits of rocks rained down as the men made their way

down the cliff face. Luke leaned over Megan to protect her, as much as he could, from the assault. Moments later, the rescuers reached them and Luke moved aside to allow them access to Megan.

They checked her vital signs, placed a cervical collar around her neck, bandaged her head wound, then gently slid her onto the litter and prepared her for transport up the cliff. Luke knew a little about mountain rescue techniques, having been involved in one years before when a hiker had fallen while climbing one of the Fourteeners surrounding the town. Some of the fourteen-thousand-foot peaks were a relatively easy hike, but others were more of a test. Every summer climbers got into difficulty trying to bag one. Thanks to the rescue squad's efforts, most survived. The titanium litter had a four-point webbing configuration with the main line attached to Megan and the belay line attached to the medic. Ever so slowly, they raised her up the face of the cliff.

Twelve tense minutes later, all of them were back on safe ground. One of the paramedics checked Megan over again before she was settled in the ambulance.

"Gil's been apprehended and will be charged with attempted murder," Matt told Luke as he waited impatiently while the medic examined Megan. "The rest of his crimes will be investigated fully and I've got a feeling we weren't the only victims of his embezzling. Gil won't be seeing the outside of a jail cell for many, many years to come."

Luke knew Matt's words were meant to comfort him, but Megan hadn't regained consciousness. He turned away from Matt, wanting to hide his distress from his brother, and saw Cody waiting by his SUV. He'd never seen anyone look so forlorn in his life. He strode over to his son and hugged him, trying to impart hope and strength.

"Will she..." Cody sobbed against his shoulder.

"She'll be fine, son. She's a fighter, remember that."

"She sure is," Cody told him, and Luke could hear the pride in his voice.

"I...love you, Cody," Luke told him, needing his son to know he truly did.

"I love you, too, Dad," Cody said, his voice breaking with emotion.

They held on to each other until the medic came over to see if Luke had any injuries, but he waved him away.

"Let's get going," he said. They climbed in beside Megan, and moments later, they were heading back down the mountain, toward the hospital in Silver Springs.

LUKE HELD MEGAN'S HAND on the ride to the hospital, praying her injuries weren't severe. She still hadn't regained consciousness and that bothered him. If only he'd driven faster, he might have gotten to Inspiration Point before Gill pushed her off the cliff.

He felt so impotent, he wanted to find Gil and punch his lights out. With any luck, maybe one of the other inmates down at the county jail would do it for him.

"Luke?"

He glanced down at Megan. "Hey," he whispered, unable to get more than a single word out of his dry throat.

"You looked so angry," she said softly.

He stroked her forehead. "Just thinking about what I'd like to do to Gil. None of it pretty."

She smiled and said, "My hero." Then she passed out again.

Epilogue

Eight weeks later, Megan and Luke finally got to repeat their wedding vows again, this time in front of their family and friends. That evening, after the guests had departed, Megan sat in the living room with the girls, remembering the past two months as Luke collected their bags.

The guest list had swelled considerably in the ensuing weeks and now included all the rescue and medical personnel involved in Megan's rescue and her hospital care. She'd been delighted to see them and thank them personally for everything they'd done for her.

She'd suffered from a subdural hematoma as a result of her fall and had been operated on that night. She'd also dislocated her shoulder, grabbing at the rock face as she fell. Had she not done so, she wouldn't have landed on the ledge—but *that* had resulted in two broken ankles. However, those injuries were a small price to pay to save her from certain death.

Luke hadn't left Megan's side during her hospital stay, but the most surprising visitor was Sasha, who'd insisted on helping with her recovery by reading to her from the newspaper and then, when Megan was up to it, doing crosswords together.

There was a surprise appearance—her parents and brother. Luke admitted, minutes before they were due to walk down the aisle, that he'd invited them. They'd been formal with her but their manner had thawed under the O'Malley charm, mostly Will's. He'd encouraged them to reconcile with her and get to know their grandson. It remained to be seen if they'd take any further interest in Cody's life…or Megan's. Right now, she was too happy to care.

There were still gaps in Megan's memory, mostly relating to when she'd first confronted Gil. In many ways, she was thankful she couldn't remember being pushed over the cliff. Whenever Megan thought of it, she felt sick to her stomach.

Apparently, she'd had the wherewithal to give Luke a clue as to where she was, but had no memory of their phone conversation.

She'd also lost a lot of blood from a gash on her temple sustained during her fall. Sasha had apparently been the first to offer her own blood for transfusion. She smiled at the thought and the probable frown on Sasha's face when she'd been turned down as too young to donate.

"Megan?"

She looked up into Sasha's eyes and smiled. "I was just thinking about you." She patted the sofa beside her.

Sasha took a seat and asked, "Are you okay? Today hasn't been too tiring, has it?"

Megan smiled again and stroked Sasha's blond hair. "No, honey, it's been a great day. Thank you for agreeing to be one of my bridesmaids."

Sasha grinned. "You gotta admit I look better in a dress than Daisy does."

"Well, as I've never seen your sister in a dress, I'll have to take your word for it. You looked so pretty. Like a princess—"

"Me, too, Mommy!" Celeste shouted. She bounced onto the sofa, earning a glance of reproach from her older sister.

Megan tickled her. "You, my little pumpkin, looked like a fairy princess!"

"Really?"

"Uh-huh."

"Too bad Daisy didn't want to look pretty."

"She did in her own way, standing up with her father and brother," Megan assured her.

"That's just plain weird, a girl wanting to be on the groom's side of the wedding," Sasha muttered.

Megan couldn't help laughing. "I think she looked just right in her new cowboy boots and jeans. She matched her father and her brother and uncles perfectly," she said. This time around, Luke had forsaken the tuxedos for clothing more suited for the ranch. Megan had already admired the digital photos taken of the wedding party, with the men—and Daisy—attired in cowboy boots, jeans, chambray shirts and cowboy hats, while the bride's party wore floral summery dresses that drifted in the breeze.

They'd said their vows beside the lake that stretched between the ranch house and the mountains that rose behind it. Megan couldn't imagine a more idyllic setting.

"You look happy."

She gazed up into Luke's warm brown eyes and moved over on the sofa to make room for him.

He squeezed into the space between Megan and Celeste and placed a noisy kiss on Megan's lips.

"Gross!" Daisy and Cody both said from the doorway into the living room.

Smiling, Luke repeated it. Megan giggled and Sasha leaped off the sofa. "Old people sex!" she squealed and ran from the room with her hands over her eyes.

"What's old people sex?" Celeste asked as she watched them curiously.

"Nothing you need to worry about for a very long time," Luke said, then kissed her forehead.

Always curious, she asked, "How long? Next week?"

"Long after next week, darlin'," Luke told his youngest daughter as she climbed off the sofa and went to join her siblings.

"Speaking of old people sex," Luke murmured in Megan's ear. "Shall we head off on our honeymoon?"

Megan pushed at his chest. "I can't believe I agreed to go camping on horseback for our honeymoon. I must still be concussed."

"You're the one who didn't want to venture too far from the kids," he said.

"True. But—"

Luke silenced her protests with another kiss. When they both came up for air, he said, "Remind me what a bad idea it is when I make love to you tonight on a carpet of meadow grass sprinkled with wildflowers beneath a star-studded sky."

"I'm not sure which will take my breath away more, the scenery—or your lovemaking," she teased.

Luke stood and pulled her to her feet." The sooner we leave, the sooner you'll find out."

LATER THAT EVENING, satiated and happier than she could have ever dreamed, Megan lay in Luke's arms looking up at the starry sky.

Luke rolled toward her and nuzzled her ear. "Well?" he asked. "Which took your breath away more?"

Megan turned in his arms. "You know, I can't quite decide," she murmured. "I need some time to think about it."

"Take all the time you want, darlin'," Luke drawled. "We've got the rest of our lives."

* * * * *